*What do you do when your bratty brother
turns your meanest aunt into a monster?*

Green lightning flashed from Denny, through Aunt Matty, to T.E., and to Bunkie. There was a hissing, growling roar, like all the lions in the zoo at once . . . A light like a star flooded the kitchen. Aunt Matty, the bird, my cat, and Denny were swallowed up in a blinding light.

Then the supernatural light disappeared. I couldn't move. My eyes bugged out. Aunt Matty, the cat, and the parakeet were gone. And a *real* griffin crouched on our kitchen floor!

Don't miss Natalie and Denny
in their next two Magical Mysteries
WHITE MAGIC
and
NEXT DOOR WITCH

"A delightful new series, with a pair of charming but flawed kids who act like real siblings, save that they keep stumbling into genuine magic . . . Seasoned with a hint of deeper mysticism, this is fine and lively writing that will appeal to any kid with a taste for the fantastic . . . I can't wait to see what else Mary Stanton has up her enchanted sleeve."
—Bruce Coville,
author of *My Teacher Is an Alien*

"Mary Stanton's Magical Mysteries are the stories that every child dreams of but rarely finds. Natalie and Denny have the style, pace and plots to push *Goosebumps* to the back of the rack."
—Charles Sheffield,
creator of *Jupiter Line* Young Adult Science Fiction Novels

"The Magical Mysteries are funny, exciting adventures. Magic, science, horses, kids, other worlds—what more could anyone want, at any age?"
—Nancy Kress,
author of *Oaths and Miracles*

Books in the Magical Mystery Series

MY AUNT, THE
Monster

* * * * * * *

Mary Stanton

B
BERKLEY BOOKS, NEW YORK

MY AUNT, THE MONSTER

A Berkley Book / published by arrangement with the author

PRINTING HISTORY
Berkley edition / July 1997

The Putnam Berkley World Wide Web site address is
http://www.berkley.com

ISBN: 0-425-15227-8

BERKLEY®
Berkley Books are published by The Berkley Publishing Group, 200 Madison Avenue, New York, New York 10016.
BERKLEY and the "B" design are trademarks belonging to Berkley Publishing Corporation.

PRINTED IN THE UNITED STATES OF AMERICA

10 9 8 7 6 5 4 3 2 1

THIS BOOK IS DEDICATED TO MY FRIEND BRUCE COVILLE,
WHO STARTED IT ALL

ACKNOWLEDGMENTS

To Michael Hanagan, Ph.D., of Refractron Corporation, and Paul Johnson, Ph.D., Alfred University—thanks for the lessons in thermodynamics.

To my friends Dana Paxson, Nick DiChario, and Duranna Durgin, thanks for the advice at the first-draft stage.

I would like to acknowledge my debt to the work of ''the Gentleman from Indianapolis,'' Booth Tarkington.

CHAPTER

ONE

THE PHONE RANG JUST AS THE DETERGENT COMMERCIAL came on at the end of *The Young and the Restless*. Bunkie was curled asleep at the end of my bed. She's the only cat I know who snores. I tickled her ears with her tail and let the phone ring four times because it was probably Brian Kurlander, who walked into me on purpose in the school cafeteria yesterday, and I had to be cool. At the fourth ring Bunkie woke up and flattened her ears in a way that means, "Cut it out!" I dropped her tail and picked up the receiver.

"Hello?" I said in a way that was pretty laid-back and totally cool, if I do say so myself.

"Natalie?"

"Oh. Hi, Mom."

"Are you all right?"

"I'm fine." I flopped over on my stomach and looked out my bedroom window. A big ship was steaming down the East River thirty stories down.

"You sound sort of . . . weird. Are you coming down with something?"

I coughed and went back to my regular voice. "I'm okay. Are you going to be late coming home?"

"Well, yes, sweetie. Dad, too. This meeting I'm going into will go past five. And Dad's going to be late because he's picking Aunt Matty up at the airport."

I sat straight up in bed. "Aunt Matty!" Bunkie flattened her ears in a very cross way. This cat *knows* me. I mean, it's awesome how we connect. "You mean the Griffin?"

"I mean Aunt Matty." There was a note in Mom's voice that meant, "Don't start, don't say a word, cut it out." "She's going to stay with us for the weekend. Won't that be nice?" Mom hurried on, definitely not waiting for an answer, "Where's Denny?"

"In his room, messing around."

"I want the two of you to straighten up the apartment. Make sure that Denny cleans his room. Matty will stay in his room and he can sleep on the Hide-A-Bed in the living room."

"Okay." Somebody said something in the background and Mom's voice faded off the phone for a second. She and Dad are partners in an advertising agency. She's really successful at business, but she's not real focused on the domestic, if you know what I mean. "Natalie?"

"Right here, Mom."

"When you've finished cleaning up, you and Denny go down to Mr. Feather and get some egg rolls and fried rice for dinner. Enough for six, sweetie. You know how Matty eats. Tell Denny he can get some cuttlefish for T. E."

That stupid bird. "Can I get some shrimp for Bunkie, then?"

"Shrimp? For the cat? Of course not, sweetie. Bunkie can have leftovers. Just tell Mr. Feather to put it on the bill. Be sure to order some vegetables."

"Uh-huh."

"Love you. We'll all be home around eight."

"Love you, Mom."

I hung up the phone and hollered, "Denny!"

No answer. I clicked off the TV. The apartment was quiet. "DennNEE!"

Still no answer. Brat. Of all the little brothers to have, Denny has got to be the worst. I've mentioned this to Mom, strictly in the spirit of giving her useful information, and she just groans, rolls her eyes, and says stuff like "Why can't you two get along?" and "You'll appreciate each other more when you're both older." She'll even drag the photo album from the bookshelf and take out pictures of the two of us in the bathtub at age six and zero or something. She says it's the two of us, but I don't believe it. Denny was never that defenseless.

"Darn it, Denny. Come here!"

Bunkie sat up abruptly. Denny appeared at my bedroom door, his stupid parakeet, T. E., on his shoulder. Now, some people, like Mrs. Murchinson on the twenty-third floor and old Mrs. Feather at the Silver Feather Deli downstairs, think that Denny is adorable. I guess he has your basic cute-kid equipment. Freckles. Red hair that sticks up in all directions. But behind all that is a devil in a kid suit. You've gotta know him.

"What?" said Denny. T. E. hopped from his head to his shoulder. A boy and his bird. Denny had gotten this parakeet when we moved from Milwaukee to New York City because Mom and Dad said Denny needed a pet. You can't have a dog in New York, at least not in a forty-story condo. So Denny got this bird, which Dad called T. E. It's initials for The Eagle, which was the kind of bird Denny really wanted.

"Mom says to clean your room."

T. E. chirped and Denny said, "It *is* clean," which of course it wasn't.

"Clean enough for Aunt Matty to stay in it?"

Denny's eyes got big. "Aunt Matty's coming?"

"For the weekend. We have to clean up the place and then go get dinner from Mr. Feather's."

"How long is she going to stay?"

"I told you. Till Monday."

Denny clutched his stomach and groaned in this hyper-spazz way. T. E. launched himself into the air, flew around in a circle, and landed on Bunkie's head. She growled and lashed her tail.

"Get that bird off my cat and let's get going. There's a bunch of stuff to do."

"Aunt Matty can't stay until Monday!" Denny said. "Aunt Matty hates kids! Besides, I've got Little League in the park tomorrow. Aunt Matty hates baseball more than she hates kids. And if she won't come to the game, Mom won't come."

"No," I agreed gloomily. "She'll make Mom take her shopping. And she'll make me go, too. And I was going roller skating. At least, I'm pretty sure I'm going roller skating."

"With Bri-ann," said Denny, making this stupid face. "Woo-ooo-woo, Bri-ANN."

"Shut up, Denny. Mom and Dad'll be home at eight and we've got stuff to do."

"Does *she* have to stay in my room? Why doesn't *she* stay in your room? And where am I supposed to sleep?"

"You'll sleep on the Hide-A-Bed."

"T. E. hates the Hide-A-Bed. It's got this big lump in the middle. Why doesn't Aunt Matty sleep on the Hide-A-Bed?"

"Because it's got a lump in the middle."

"I'm gonna quarelltine my room."

"Quarantine," I said. "You can't quarantine your room because that means there's a communicable disease contaminating it. The only contamination is all that dirty underwear."

Denny opened his mouth to whine, and I said, "Just cool it and get this stuff done before they get here."

Then the doorbell and the phone rang at exactly the same time. I watched the phone, counting the rings. This had to be Brian Kurlander. Maybe he wanted to go to the movies instead of roller skating. "Answer the door, Denny."

"I'm not supposed to answer the door by myself. Mom said not to. Not in New York."

Maybe the person at the door wouldn't mind waiting in the hall just a little bit. I counted the phone rings: three . . . four rings. The doorbell rang again. Whoever was out there sounded mad. I picked up the phone.

"Hello?" I said into the receiver.

"Natalie?"

It was Dad. Great.

"Is that the doorbell I hear in the background?"

"Yeah, Dad. The doorbell and phone rang at the same time."

"That'll be Matty, honey. I had to ask her to take a cab from the airport. Mom and I have to take these new clients to dinner. We may be going to Paris! I've explained it all to Matty and gave her a key to the lobby. So you three have a good time until we get home, all right? It's going to be late, so you'll be in bed before we get there. I'll see you in the morning. There's the bell again. Don't leave Matty standing in the hall.''

Jeez!

I hung up. Looked at Denny. Denny looked at me. ''She's here,'' I said, ''And Mom and Dad won't be home until late.''

''You mean we're going to be alone with her?'' Denny's eyes bugged out. You're probably wondering what's so awful about Aunt Matty. She's not that bad. If you don't mind Godzilla for an aunt. I'll bet you've seen the magazine cover of Aunt Matty, the one without the fur coat, where she's sitting in a fancy office with a bunch of scared-looking guys in suits standing behind her. What she is, is the president of Griffin Corporation. And what a griffin is, actually, is a mythical monster with the head of an eagle, the body of a lion, and the tail of a dragon or serpent. Very good description of Aunt Matty, Dad says, when Mom isn't around to hear him. Her real job name is CEO, which Dad says is a set of initials for Chief Executive Officer. I say it's initials for Children Exterminated Often. The magazine story called her ''the Dragon of Wall Street.'' Honest to gosh.

I opened the front door and there was Aunt Matty, my mom's sister. Otherwise known as Madeline Carmichael. She stood in the hallway looking a little shorter than Godzilla, but not much.

''Good heavens, Natalie. What took you so long?''

This wasn't really a question. Just Aunt Matty being

cross. She stomped into the apartment, wearing one of her coats made from the fur of some poor animal she probably caught and tortured herself.

Anyhow, there was the Griffin herself standing in our apartment, ready to torture us kids all weekend. She slung her coat into the closet and whomped her suitcase onto the floor. "Well, children. I've been elected to baby-sit until your parents get home."

Children, right!?

She looked around the living room, hands on her hips. "This place is a mess. We'll get it shipshape and then I'll make something for you two to eat."

I figured a small fib was essential. "Uh. Mom's asked us to get food from the Silver Feather Deli, Aunt Matty. It's already ordered. All Denny and I have to do is pick it up."

"You and Denny going out? In New York City? Alone?" Aunt Matty frowned. Not that she has any other expression.

"It's just downstairs," I explained. "Denny and I get food there all the time."

"I've told both your mother and father that New York is no place to bring up children."

Children, again! This is half the problem with my mother's sister. Her brain is permanently stuck on Denny and me at about five or something. The other half of the problem is this CEO stuff. I mean, if you asked her, the fact that Aunt Matty isn't boss of the entire universe is a whatdoyacallit. Not a mistake, exactly. An oversight.

"And deli food," said Aunt Matty. "It's filled with all kinds of goodness knows what. I really ought to cook you two something healthful."

"No!" yelled Denny. "Hamburger boiled in water makes me sick!" (This is what she cooked for us the last time she was here, believe it or not.) "It makes me BARF!"

"Denny, I will not tolerate rude behavior from a six-year-old little boy. Go to your ro—"

"He's gotta help me with all those little boxes the food comes in," I said very fast. "Mom said to pick the order up right away. C'mon, Denny. We'll be back in two seconds, Aunt Matty." I jerked the kid out the front door and into the hall before he could get us into more trouble, then punched the elevator button, resisting the urge to punch Denny, too. "You bozo."

"Did you see her face?" Denny said. "She's going to kill us."

"She won't kill us, Denny." I dragged him into the elevator and hit the lobby button.

"She's gonna kill us, and Mom and Dad will come home to find our strangled bodies stuffed under the Hide-A-Bed."

The elevator stopped at the twenty-third floor. Mrs. Murchinson, the one who thinks Denny is cute, got on.

"Or maybe she'll stuff us in the Disposall," Denny went on, like the little ghoul he is, "with our blood and guts sprayed all over the kitchen."

I smiled at Mrs. Murchinson, who was looking at Denny with her face screwed up like a prune. "More likely she'll try and stuff T. E. for dinner," I said, trying to shut Denny up. This worked better than I thought. He turned so pale his freckles stood out. "Just kidding, Denny. Honestly."

"She would. I'll just bet she would. And parakeet's healthful, right? Like chicken."

"I didn't mean it, Denny. It was just a joke." The elevator finally got to the lobby and I shoved Denny out.

The Silver Feather Deli is the best part of the building where we live. For one thing, it smells great. And when you walk in, these little silver bells over the door ring for good luck. Old Mrs. Feather, Mr. Feather's mom, sits right behind the cash register to take your money. Past the cash register, there's shelves and shelves of strange stuff: green and blue bottles with powders and spices; little packages wrapped in streaky white paper tied with red string; big clear glass bottles with corks in the tops and funny wrinkled fruit inside. What's even better is the magic. People can get more than deli food here, they say, if they know just what to ask old Mrs. Feather.

Mr. Feather, who is old Mrs. Feather's son, is the one who does all the cooking, and the stuff is good. They are American Indians. Mr. Feather speaks just like us, but old Mrs. Feather doesn't say much English. She's about a hundred years old, I guess, and remembers the days when she lived on a reservation in, like, Arizona or somewhere. I asked her if he was around so I could give him our order.

"Ha-ho," she said, or something like that, and her son came out from the kitchen.

"Hey, Natalie, what's happening? Denny. How's it going, my man? How's T. E.?"

"The Griffin's here," said Denny, like he was some kind of major accident victim, "and she's going to kill T. E. unless we get some deli food quick."

"Kill T. E.?" said old Mrs. Feather, her gray eyebrows rising up.

"Nobody's going to kill T. E.," I said, "It's just that the Griffin, I mean Aunt Matty, is here, and Denny's being a bozo, Mrs. Feather. Mr. Feather, we'd like four servings of fried rice and a double order of butterfly shrimp.'' I thought of Bunkie, that good old cat, "Make that a triple order of butterfly shrimp.''

"And vegetables?'' said Mr. Feather.

"Vegetables. Right.'' I sighed.

"Griffin?'' said old Mrs. Feather to her son. Then she said something so fast that I couldn't figure it out at all.

"A monster, Ma. A lion, an eagle, and a dragon. What about some soup, Natalie?''

I ordered soup. Mr. Feather went away to cook our food. Denny chattered away to old Mrs. Feather and I wandered around looking at all the cool things in the store.

Back in the elevator, Denny held on to the food I'd given him to carry without saying a single thing. Usually it's hard to shut my little brother up. I shifted the bags I was carrying. "What's up, Denny?''

He looked at me. "Old Mrs. Feather gave me some stuff.''

"What kind of stuff?''

"Good-luck stuff. To keep the Griffin from stuffing T. E. for dinner.''

I wondered if Denny was ever going to get some sense or if I was going to spend my whole life keeping him in the real world. "I was kidding, Denny. It was just a joke.''

In the time we'd been gone to the Silver Feather Deli, Aunt Matty had cleaned up the living room, vacuumed it, folded out the Hide-A-Bed, put Denny's Power Rangers sheets on it, and set the table. When we came in, she was walking around the living room with her portable phone glued to her ear, snapping into it like an alligator on those *National Geographic* specials Dad makes us watch. She opened the front door wider with her free hand and waved us into our own home, for Pete's sake.

"Buy Aerostar," she said into the phone, or something like that, and then, "and kill the"—here she said a *very* rude word, which Dad won't let me write, even though I hear it in school all the time—"son of a *word* who thinks it's worth more."

"Where's T. E.?" Denny said in a worried voice, picking up on Aunt Matty's advice to kill.

Aunt Matty waved at him to shush.

"Where's my BIRD!" Denny howled. "Where's my parakeet? WHERE's T. E.!"

Aunt Matty clapped her hand over the phone and glared. "Quiet! Kitchen! Oven!"

"Aaaaggh!" Denny yelled.

I followed the little sucker into the kitchen, and there was T. E., of course, sitting in front of the oven on top of Bunkie's head and my good old cat was taking it, like always. "See, Denny? The Eagle's just fine. Now help me unpack this stuff."

He totally ignored me, naturally. Just slammed the bag of rice on the floor and knelt down in front of his bird. He dug into his jeans pocket and brought out one of the packets of streaky white paper tied with red string and a little silver bell.

"Denny. Cut that out and help me with the food."

Denny unfolded the paper. A small pile of greeny-gold powder glimmered in the middle. Denny shook it into the palm of his hand. Then, still kneeling, he bowed to one corner of the kitchen, turned on his knees, and bowed to the next corner, then the next, until he'd bowed to each corner.

T. E. chirped.

Bunkie meowed.

Except for my bossy aunt Matty yelling on the phone in the next room and my little brother worshiping the appliances, everything was normal.

Until . . .

"Hai yung HAI!" said Denny, and threw the greeny-gold powder over Bunkie and T. E.

"Hey!" I said.

"Hai yung HAI!" Denny said again, and rang the silver bell. The powder floated above the cat and the bird in a little cloud.

Denny rang the silver bell a second time. The powder swirled like a cake batter in a mixer, around and around, faster and faster until Denny's bird and my cat were both hidden in a glittery curtain.

I dropped the bags and jumped forward. "Denny," I yelled. "Stop that."

There was a miniature crash of thunder. Aunt Matty whomped into the kitchen, hollering, "What in the *world* is going on in here?" She marched over to Denny, grabbed him by the scruff of the neck with one hand, and reached down to grab T. E. with the other.

The thunder rolled again. And then . . . it was awesome. A piece of green lightning flashed from Denny, through Aunt Matty, to T. E., and to Bunkie. There was a hissing, growling roar, like all the lions in the zoo at once. The powder spiraled up like a whirlwind. Denny wriggled away from Aunt Matty with his lower lip stuck out and rang the bell a third time. The powder exploded. A light like a star flooded the kitchen. Aunt Matty, the bird, my cat, and

Denny were swallowed up in a blinding light so white that everything disappeared.

The supernatural light disappeared. Denny stood there, his face all covered with powder.

I couldn't move. My toes had grown into the floor like tree roots. My eyes bugged out. Aunt Matty, the cat, and the parakeet were gone. And a *real* griffin crouched on our kitchen floor!

My breath was stuck somewhere down around my stomach. I was so scared I swallowed my spit the wrong way and choked. I crouched down and stared at the griffin.

At least the monster wasn't big. It was just about the size of T. E. and Bunkie together, with the head of an eagle and the body of a small, powerful lion. I crawled forward a little, still staring. The eagle head was kind of beautiful, with white feathers on top and brown and black feathers around the big gold eyes. The body was gruesome. Those claws were fierce, with curved talons like silvery swords. Instead of a regular lion's tail, it had a nasty-looking spike at the end, like pictures of devils in Denny's Spiderman comic books.

"Wow," said Denny.

"Shut UP!" I hissed, scared that it'd jump us.

"Where's Aunt Matty?" Denny asked, looking around. "And T. E.? Where's my BIRD?"

I smacked my hand over Denny's mouth.

Everything was quiet. The griffin just stood there. Then it gave a long, long howl and made a sound like cats fighting in the backyard of our house in Milwaukee, where I wished both Denny and I were right this minute.

"It ate her. We made a monster and it ate her," said Denny in an interested way.

And what did he mean *we*? I didn't have a darn thing to do with this. "Maybe Aunt Matty ran into the living room and we just didn't see her. You follow me, Dennis Ross, and stay away from the *thing*." We backed into the living room. Keeping Denny behind me, I turned around in a circle, looking at the living room bit by bit. Nope, she wasn't on the sofa. Nope, she wasn't under the sofa. And there weren't any feet in high-heeled shoes behind the curtains.

Aunt Matty wasn't there.

"Aunt Matty?" My voice didn't come out as loud as I thought it would, so I said, louder, "AUNT MATTY?"

Silence, except for *skritch-skritch-skritch* from the kitchen.

"I told you. It ate her," said Denny.

I went to the coat closet. Opened it. Looked down at the closet floor. There was Aunt Matty's suitcase and her fur coat. I cracked open our front door and poked my head into the hallway. Empty. I closed the door and locked it.

There was a *click-click-click* of clawed feet walking on linoleum. The noise stopped as it hit the rug in the living room.

I turned around. The griffin stared at me, its beak opening and shutting with a powerful snap. Its little beady eyes winked back at me, flat, black, and evil.

I stared at my little brother. How could he do this?

Then the phone rang.

CHAPTER

two

"EeerrEEW!" went the griffin.

Now this should tell you how totally bummed out I was: I didn't care if it was Brian Kurlander on the phone or not. All I wanted was for that stupid phone to shut up so I could concentrate.

The phone kept on ringing. The answering machine kicked in and I heard Dad's recorded voice saying, "You have reached the residence of Alison and David Ross. No one is available to answer your call right now, so please leave your name, number, and the time of your call" and then Dad's live voice after the beep saying, "Natalie? Are you there? Can you pick up?"

Denny yelled, "Dad!" and picked up the phone.

I grabbed it out of his sweaty little hand before he could blow the whole thing. "Um. Dad? Hi."

"Hi, honey. How's it going?"

"Fine, Dad, fine."

"Is Matty there?"

15

"Not ex—"

"EeGAK!" went the griffin.

I must have jumped a foot, but I recovered pretty fast. "—actly. I mean, not right now."

"Did she arrive and go out again?"

The griffin marched around the living room, poking its head into things with a sort of a tippy-toed swagger. Aunt Matty's purse was on the floor next to the couch. It stuck its head inside. Then it hopped up around some more, fluttered its wings, and flew onto the windowsill. It looked at its reflection in the glass and shrieked, "SQWAAA!"

"Natalie!"

"Yes, Dad."

"What's that noise? Where's Matty? What's going on? I—excuse me just a second, honey." He talked to someone near the phone in the kind of impatient way you get when somebody's bugging you and you want to pay attention to something else. Sorta like me and this griffin with Dad on the other end of the line. I thought fast. I thought hard. I couldn't think of a thing to do except watch this griffin to make sure it didn't eat us.

Denny, abnormally quiet, had stuck his thumb in his mouth and was looking at the griffin. The Thing swiveled its head and looked at me with one glittering cold eye.

Dad came back on the line. "Can you put Denny on the kitchen extension? Mom and I need to talk to you."

"Uh, sure. Hang on, Dad." I covered the bottom of the phone with my hand. The last thing I needed was Denny messing things up with his version of how he'd turned his bird, my cat, and my mom's sister into a griffin. Because there was no doubt in my mind that's what had happened. Its body was Bunkie-colored: gray with streaks of cream and brown. But where Bunkie had nice delicate paws and a slim body, this thing was muscley with the blunt thick claws of a lion. T. E. had the same beady black eyes, but the parakeet's thin round skull covered with yellow feathers had been replaced by a big powerful head and a lockjaw beak.

As far as the Aunt Matty part? A couple of pigeons whizzed by the window and the griffin screeched like a buzz saw. What happened next proved Aunt Matty was in that griffin because it slammed right into the glass after that pigeon like Aunt Matty telling her business guys to kill that son of a *word*.

The phone was practically vibrating to death in my hand, what with Dad yelling and all. I uncovered it and put it back to my ear.

". . . GOING ON?'' Dad shouted. "We can't take this trip, Alison. It's not going to work. We can't leave the kids for that long and I refuse—''

"Just settle down, dear. Natalie?'' It was Mom, on one of the office extensions.

"Hi, Mom.''

"Natalie, we're going to Paris!''

"Paris? Paris, France?''

"It's the biggest chance the agency's had ever since we opened!'' She sounded like it was Christmas. "And we're going tomorrow!''

"Tomorrow? Paris?''

"It's the largest account we've ever handled. It just came in this afternoon. I still can't believe it. I keep thinking that something will happen to keep us from going.''

Right. Like this monster bird hopping around the carpet.

"Anyway, Dad and I have made plans we need to talk to you about. Is Matty there?"

"Ah. She's out right now." Like, out of body.

"Well, we'll tell her everything when we get home to-night. Dad and I are taking an Air France flight to Paris tomorrow morning. We'll be gone for three weeks. Dad and I discussed it, and we thought we'd send you and Denny to Uncle Bart's. Would you like that?"

"Uncle Bart's? We're going to Uncle Bart's?"

Denny, hearing the Uncle Bart part of the conversation yelled "YAY!" because he loves it at Uncle Bart's. Uncle Bart is my mom's youngest brother and he lives on this totally cool horse farm in upstate New York. We stay there summers, usually.

"Things are going to happen really fast, honey," Mom said. "We've hired a tutor to take you and Denny up to the horse farm tomorrow. She's the sister of our reception-ist, and a graduate student, so she'll be able to keep you guys up with your studies. Oh!" She laughed. "I can't believe this is happening! You don't mind, Natalie? You like Bart, and we'll be back soon."

"Are you coming home tonight?"

"Of course we are! I want to tell you and Matty all about it. We'll be late, sweetie, so don't wait up for us. Love you."

"Love you," I said in this hollow kind of way. I hung up the phone. Looked at Denny. "They're going to Paris," I said. "We're going to Uncle Bart's."

"Wow."

"Don't you 'wow' me, Dennis Ross. You bring Aunt Matty back right now. And my cat. I want my cat!"

"You do it," said Denny, scowling.

"I wasn't the one that did it in the first place, was I, stupid? *I* wasn't the one that flapped her lip to old Mrs. Feather. *I* wasn't the smart guy." I took a deep breath, ready to yell some more, and Denny's lip stuck out and his face turned red. I had a sudden, awful feeling, sort of like finding out there's no floor in an elevator. I breathed hard to clear my head. I grabbed Denny by the front of his Terminator T-shirt. It had I'LL BE BACK written on it. Right. "Denny. You don't know how to get them back, do you?"

"Let go of my shirt!"

I hung on and thought a minute. The griffin swiveled its head toward us, and looked at Denny like it'd looked at the pigeon. I dragged Denny to the front door. "We gotta get out of here."

"Where are we going?"

"The Silver Feather Deli, of course." I should have thought of it right away. "Mrs. Feather knew how to make a griffin. She should be able to unmake it."

Right on the first count. Wrong on the second. When we got to the deli, Mr. Feather had gone somewhere and old Mrs. Feather was all by herself at the cash register. I figured this was just as well, since Mr. Feather was good friends with my folks and I didn't want anyone else to know about the griffin.

"Mrs. Feather," I said, "um. We've got a problem." Old Mrs. Feather bowed to me. I bowed back, to be polite. "That stuff you gave Denny? You know, the griffin stuff?"

"Griffin," said old Mrs. Feather. "Yes, ah, yes." She sort of sucked in her breath when she did this, which Mom says is part of being old sometimes. I didn't know whether I should suck, too, to be polite, but I figured maybe it'd help. "The, ah, griffin, Mrs. Feather. Can we, ah, may we have T. E. and Bunkie, ah, back?'' I stopped sucking, since I was getting dizzy. "The spell, you know, that you gave Denny. We need to fix it, put things back the way they were.''

"Ah yes" said Mrs. Feather. "Back."

"Please, ma'am. We've got to fix it before my mom and dad get home.''

"Ah," she said, and frowned. "You want. Cat. And bird. And Auntie.''

"Yes, ma'am."

She shook her head.

My stomach sank.

Then Mr. Feather banged in the front door. "Hey, guys," he said with his big smile, "something wrong with the food?''

I turned, bugged my eyes out at Denny to shut up, and said, "No. It's fine, delicious. Just right.''

"Did Ms. Carmichael like it?"

"You mean Aunt Matty? Um . . . she didn't get much of a chance to eat it. She got a phone call about some kind of . . .'' *Kill the son of a word,* Aunt Matty had said on the phone. "Some kind of death in her company or what-all. She had to leave.''

"The griffin ate her," said Denny, with this very satisfied look. "She's dead. Griffin food.''

Old Mrs. Feather cackled—there's no other word for it— and she and Denny started chattering like anything to each other.

"Yeah," said Denny, to old Mrs. Feather, "but I want T. E. back. And I suppose my sister wants her stupid old cat back, too.''

"Ah," she said. She turned to her son, who had opened

the cash drawer and was counting the money from the day. She rattled off a bunch of stuff in some kind of American Indian talk. Then she turned to me and gave me this very smart look, like, "Listen!"

Mr. Feather was flipping through the money, and even I could see he didn't want to be bothered. His mother gave him a sharp poke. Mr. Feather sighed and said, "My mother gets notions, you know, Natalie? She is of a very great age, which is an honorable thing in our tribe, but sometimes those of a very great age get notions." He talked back to her in Indian, and she got bossy.

"Okay, okay, Ma, but I've got to make this deposit. Can't it wait? It can't? I have to do it this now? This second? Whatever you want." He stuffed the money in a little canvas sack and said, "My mother gives you a blessing. The blessing is this. The manitou's glory is to guard . . . what, Ma?"

More Indian talk from old Mrs. Feather.

"Oh. This is for a class in school, Natalie?" He relaxed a little bit. He believes in education, just like Dad.

Mrs. Feather gave me that look.

"Yeah." I thought fast. Geography had been on my mind, lately, since I wasn't doing so well at it. "Geography."

Mr. Feather looked confused. It was a good thing he was in a hurry. "I would think it'd be more of a history subject. But . . . okay. She wants me to write it down for you so you can use it in school." He tore off a bit of cash-register paper, scribbled on it, and gave it to me. "I'm off to the bank, kids. Give my best to your mom and dad." He banged out the door again.

I read the paper. Denny poked his head around my arm and breathed into my face and read it, too.

The Manitou's spirit will leave its earthly body when it descends the Chimney to guard the Treasure at the Heart of the World in the Palm of the Hand.

This made no sense to me at all. Manitou? We had a griffin on our hands. I read it again. It still didn't make any sense.

I got this desperate feeling. I thought maybe I'd cry, but there was my incredibly dopey little brother looking up at me like I knew everything. There were my parents, taking off to Paris on this incredibly important trip just when I needed them most. There was old Mrs. Feather, smiling away, and wasn't she the one who'd listened to my little brother, which no sensible person should do? So instead of crying, I got mad. Then I thought; Who was I going to get mad at? Old Mrs. Feather, who had reached an honorable old age, like Mr. Feather said, or my brother, who never had any sense to begin with? Or my parents? Who were leaving on this big important trip when I needed them most? Getting mad wasn't going to help any more than crying would. Neither would get my cat back, or Aunt Matty.

Descends the Chimney, the paper said. I felt like throwing that stupid griffin down the chimney, if we'd had a fireplace, which we didn't.

I had to get back upstairs. It was dinnertime for Bunkie, T. E., and Aunt Matty. And I didn't want a starving griffin in my house. It might decide to eat everything in the apartment, including Denny and me.

"So now what?" said Denny.

"I don't know," I said, and all the way back up in the elevator I was, like, clueless.

The griffin wasn't in the living room, and for a second I thought maybe it had unmagicked itself while we were gone, and Bunkie and T. E. were in the kitchen, waiting to get fed. But the only thing in the kitchen was the griffin, which had either climbed or flown onto the sink. It was pecking away at the water faucet. When Denny and I came in, it whirled around and crouched squawking on the counter.

"It needs more blood," said Denny. "It's thirsty."

"Denny, it didn't get any blood. It didn't eat Aunt Matty. It *is* Aunt Matty."

Denny was right about one thing: the little monster was thirsty. I picked up Bunkie's water dish, kind of side-stepped to the sink, and put it just out of the griffin's reach. It cocked its head first to one side, then the other. The barbed tail twitched back and forth. It slunk over to the dish and scooped up some of the water in its beak, then tossed it down with a quick twist of its head. It slurped away at the water until there was barely an inch left, stretched its wings, and went, "Scraawww!"

"Denny, get me the dictionary."

"Why?"

"Because I want to look up griffins and see what they eat, that's why."

"You get it. Why do I always have to get—"

"Denny!"

I watched the griffin to make sure it wasn't going to dive-bomb me, or bash holes in the wall or anything. Denny lugged the big dictionary into the kitchen and dropped it onto the table with a thud. The griffin fluttered its wings but didn't do anything else.

"Watch out, Denny. If it moves toward us, get out of here."

Well, the dictionary wasn't much help, no matter what Dad was always saying about how useful it was for education. I learned that a griffin was a mythical monster. They got the monster part right at least. It guarded the treasures of ancient times. It had the head of an eagle, the body of a lion, and the tail of a dragon, which I could see for myself. Then I looked up *manitou,* and it said that a manitou was one of the twelve mythical spirit guardians to an Indian heaven. So much for the dictionary. So much for old Mrs. Feather's spell. Because the book said mythical for both manitous and griffins, I ditched the idea of a mystery call to a pet store. If people believed it was mythical, they weren't about to have griffin pellets for sale like they did with rabbits or hamsters.

If the stomach part was lion, I could try it on raw meat, which I knew lions ate from those darn *National Geographic* specials. But the eagle part was the head and how could the bird part chew?

I tried the griffin on T. E.'s birdseed, which it knocked off the kitchen counter with a disgusted look. Then I tried it on Bunkie's kitty kibbles, which it picked up and dropped several times like it was shopping and didn't like the sale price. I even tried the deli food to see if the Aunt Matty part would like it. The griffin got so upset it backed away and flew around the kitchen twice before it settled back next to the water dish.

I gave up and pulled the *E* part of the encyclopedia out of the bookshelf and read that eagles eat rodents for breakfast, lunch, and dinner. Live rodents, which they barf up for the baby eagles. I found out from the *R* part of the encyclopedia that in addition to being mice, rodents included moles, gophers, chipmunks, something called a vole, and rats.

This being Manhattan, there were probably rats around, except that I was pretty sure even if we went to the back alley downstairs and caught one, I couldn't feed it live to the griffin, and maybe not even if it was dead. Gross.

I was pretty tired of being educated, when it wasn't even during school hours, so I put all the encyclopedias back and pulled out the telephone directory, looked up the Bronx Zoological Gardens, and called the number. The phone rang for a long time, which make me think I was wrong about calling this late. I figured just the animal feeders would be around, and they would be the best people to ask what to feed an eagle. I sure didn't want to talk to anyone in charge who might start to ask questions. Finally the phone got picked up and this guy answered, "Zoo, yeah," and I put on this very social voice.

"I was calling inquiring about the eating habits of eagles," I said in a stuffy way. "Domesticated eagles. My brother, Dennis, is a merchant seaman and he returned from a trip to the Orient with one as a gift for me, and I was calling to inquire about its eating habits."

The stuff about the seaman and all I'd read in a story for English lit. called "The Monkey's Paw," which had been pretty cool, which is why it had stuck in my mind.

"Who the heck is this?" said the guy. "This some kinda joke? I'm busy!"

"Please!" I said. "Don't hang up."

"You kids," said the guy, "beat it."

"Mister," I said, "you have to tell me what eagles can eat. I've got one, and it's going to starve to death right in my kitchen." Right out of nowhere, I choked up, which surprised me a lot. "Please."

"Oh, all right. Raw liver will do it. Raw hamburger, too. Make sure you chop up some green stuff in it—celery, lettuce, like that. It'll need bits of bone, so try cuttlefish."

Bang. He hung up.

The eagle stew was a mess to make, but we did it. I defrosted the hamburger in the microwave and snipped up a bunch of celery with the kitchen shears. Denny even got T. E.'s cuttlefish from the bird cage and stirred some of the chips into the gunk. I mixed it in Bunkie's food dish, and we set it on the floor, because I don't care what kind of mythical monster you've got in your kitchen, it shouldn't eat off the counters.

That griffin gobbled the eagle stew down like you wouldn't believe. We finished up the deli food while it was eating, and for a minute it was kind of like it had been when good old Bunkie would eat her kitty chow right along with us at dinner. The griffin scooped up the last bit, then started to prowl around the kitchen wagging its wings and twitching its tail. Then it spotted Bunkie's litter box, marched over, scrambled around a little, and then marched back. So that took care of one worry, which was Mom finding griffin poop in the middle of the kitchen floor.

"Bring T. E.'s bird cage in here, Denny." I cut off the "why" with my best shut-up look. "It can sleep in there. You keep it in your room, anyway. It'll need a place to sleep, and you cover T. E.'s cage at night, right? That way Mom and Dad won't see it, and I'll have tomorrow to think about how we're going to get out of this mess."

The griffin didn't seem to get the idea of sleeping in the cage at all, until I figured out that it probably needed a treasure to guard. So I got the single pearl necklace I'd gotten as a birthday present a couple of years ago and stuck it on the floor of the cage. The griffin walked right in, sat down in front of it with its snaky tail curled up around its feet, and started to guard. I hoped I wouldn't have to wear the necklace soon, since getting back might be a problem.

Denny and I carried the cage to his room. Then I got him into his pajamas and tucked him in, and went to my own room and got into bed to think things over.

This was absolutely the biggest mess I'd ever been in in my life. Somehow, I had to unmagic that griffin.

I read that piece of paper with Mrs. Feather's spell on it over at least a zillion times, until I had it memorized.

The Manitou's spirit will leave its earthly body when it descends the Chimney to guard the Treasure at the Heart of the World in the Palm of the Hand.

Maybe I could talk again to Mrs. Feather and straighten her out about the difference between griffins and manitous. But first—I had to get us a little time. Mom and Dad would want to know where Aunt Matty was. I got up, went to the hall closet, got her coat and suitcase, and stuck them in my room under the bed. Then I wrote a note.

Dear Mom and Dad,
    Aunt Matty had to take a trip. She'll be back soon. She said she is sorry to leave, but it's an emergency. We ate all the vegetables from the Silver Feather Deli.

I had to study geography all night so I'll be pretty tired
when you get home.

Love, Natalie

I stuck the note on the refrigerator, then added:

P.S. Aunt Matty said raw hamburger stew was healthy.
We will eat it tomorrow. DO NOT THROW OUT!

Then I got into bed, turned out the light, and tried to
think of a way out of this mess. But all I could see was
my little brother in the middle of green lightning. I dreamed
about that all night, practically, seeing Denny like I'd never
seen him before.

Next thing I knew, Mom was in my room getting me up
for breakfast.

"I'm very upset," Mom said over oatmeal and grapefruit
juice at the table, "Matty just taking off like that."

"Don't slurp your oatmeal, Denny," I said. "She had
an emergency at the office, Mom. There was some death
there, or something, I think."

"A death? Someone died?"

"Aunt Matty killed someone," Denny said helpfully. "I
heard her say so on the phone. Kill him, she said."

"But *still,*" said Mom, "leaving Natalie and Denny
alone like that!"

"It wasn't for very long," said Dad, and he gave Mom
this *look,* which means "not in front of the children," so
she didn't say anything more. "Well, she's gone," said
Dad cheerfully, "and it's almost seven-thirty, honey."

Mom looked at her watch, "My gosh, so it is. You two
are going to have to get ready."

Denny banged his spoon on his dish of oatmeal like he was three years old.

"We thought," said Mom, "that you and Denny could go up to the lake on Amtrak, as we usually do, since you like the train so much, and you can take Bunkie in her carrier."

I hoped that the griffin liked trains. "Yeah," I said, "and?"

"And the tutor will be here in about an hour."

"What's her name?" Maybe this tutor could be trusted with the secret of the griffin.

"Althea Brinker. Her sister brought her to one of our office parties, and she'll be very good for you."

"How old is she?" I said, getting suspicious that maybe this person was not going to be cool after all. I mean, *good for you* can mean a lot of different things to adults. Like brussels sprouts are good for you. Going to the dentist and getting your teeth mangled with a metal drill is good for you.

"Nineteen. She went through undergraduate school in just two years," said Mom.

"She graduated high school two years early," said Dad. "Brilliant girl."

"She's in a very challenging master's program at NYU," said Mom. "You're both going to like her a lot."

I didn't. And it wasn't because I got all hyperspazz rushing around packing, and calling my best friend, Nan, to say good-bye, and writing a letter to Brian Kurlander with Uncle Bart's address so he could write or call anytime. It wasn't even because I was worried about taking that griffin up to Uncle Bart's—it'd be a lot easier to figure out what to do there than it would be in Manhattan, since Uncle Bart was easy on us kids and didn't much care what we did as long as we didn't get into trouble.

I didn't like Althea Brinker because she was a dweeb. A tall bossy dweeb, who was going to be more trouble than Aunt Matty and Denny put together.

CHAPTER

three

MOM WAS SITTING ON THE COUCH WITH DENNY ON HER lap talking to me when Althea Brinker buzzed her way into my life. We were all packed. I'd just found Mom's passport for her in the clean-clothes basket in the laundry room. Once Mom had her passport, everything was cool, and everybody stopped being hyperspazz. I opened the door after the second buzz and said hi. Althea *looked* okay. A little skinny, maybe, and very pale from all that studying indoors, but her jacket was totally cool and the glasses she wore were neat: big with red rims. And her hair was definitely awesome, being red and long with lots of curls.

"You must be Natalie?"

"Yeah. Come on in."

She said hi and shook hands with Mom and Dad and crouched down to shake hands with Denny.

"We're so grateful that you could help us out on short notice," said Mom, when everybody had settled down. "I've got the Amtrak tickets, our itinerary in Paris, with

31

phone numbers where we can be reached, and a list of the doctors and dentists Natalie and Denny use when they're at my brother's place. If you need more cash than we gave you, just ask my brother Bart. He'll keep accounts for us. He also has the permission slips for medical treatment if anything should happen.''

"Great," said Althea Brinker. "I stopped by the school this morning with the permission slip you gave me and talked to Natalie and Denny's teachers to find out where they are in their studies.'' She dug into her backpack and brought out this yellow pad. "Educationally speaking, Denny's doing really well.'' She frowned a little. "Natalie got pink-slipped in geography, so we're going to have to concentrate on some special areas. I've made a list.''

"Pink-slipped?" said Dad. "You mean an unsatisfactory notice?''

The first time we had gone to Uncle Bart's place on Cayuga Lake, I'd run right down to the dock and jumped in without sticking my toe in the water to see how cold it was. Talk about a shock. I felt like that now. Just like I'd been punched in the stomach. The thing about this pink slip was I forgot to give it to my folks. I'd gotten an A in geography the semester before, then Brian Kurlander moved to Manhattan and sat right in front of me in this class at the beginning of second semester, and I got distracted. I was so embarrassed that I went to Mrs. Holmes, the teacher, asked how I could make up some stuff, and I was already working on bringing that grade back up. But good old Detective Althea must have checked the school records. And here she goes and rats on me to my folks. She could have asked me, first.

I decided immediately that I wouldn't have red curly hair

if you paid me a million dollars. Even if it was in cash, in unmarked bills.

"Natalie. What's this?" said Dad. "Your last report card showed A's and B's." He looked at Althea Brinker. "I'm afraid I don't understand."

"I don't think it's a big deal, Mr. Ross," said Althea the fink. "From a learning standpoint, I'm sure that with the proper amount of studying, Natalie will be fine."

Educationally speaking? I couldn't *stand* this!

Long silence. A BIG long silence. Then Dad said to me, "Well?"

"Um," I said. "Um. The pink slip's in my drawer. I just didn't have a whole lot of time to show it to you guys. The way I've been studying geography to catch up and all."

Well, there was the usual, "Why didn't you tell us?" and "I thought we had an atmosphere of trust in this family," and I was feeling worse and worse about not showing that unsatisfactory report to Mom and Dad.

"I'm sorry," I said. I mean what with my good old cat Bunkie turned into the hind end of a mythical monster, and most of the rest of the monster being Aunt Matty, a person had a lot on her mind, but I couldn't tell them that. "I really just forgot."

"And she really is doing better," said Althea Brinker with a smug, snarky, cheesy smile. "We'll talk geography all the way up to Cayuga Lake on the train."

Swell. I was going to tell this person about the griffin?

"We love you, sweetie," said Mom with a sigh. "Next time just let us know, okay?"

"No harm done, I guess," said Dad. "Natalie, I assume

that you took T. E. down to old Mrs. Feather. Is Bunkie packed up in the cat carrier?''

If I answered the question about T. E., it was going to be two major fibs in a week, which is way past my limit. ''I'll go see to Bunkie, now, Dad.''

I jerked my head at Denny to follow me. We went into his room and I shut the door. I was boiling.

''Geography all the way up on the train,'' I said. ''This is the worst. 'Educationally speaking'! Gaack! Can you believe we're going to have to spend a month with that person? A whole month?'' I took a deep breath. ''Did you feed it this morning?''

''Yeah.''

''What's it doing?''

Denny went over to the cage in the corner and pulled the cover off. The griffin was sitting on its hind end in front of the pearl necklace. It woke when the light hit its little beady eyes, and blinked at me.

''SceerAW!'' said the griffin. ''Heeerrrp!''

''SHH!'' I hissed.

''Heeerrp. Heerrp. HERRP!''

''Hey!'' said Denny. He squatted down and poked at the griffin.

''Heeerp! HEERRP!''

''Oh, no,'' I said. It sounded like . . . I knew what it sounded like: Help. Help. Help. ''Denny. Denny. It's talking!''

''Cool!''

My hands felt like they'd been stuck in a snowbank for a million years. I squatted beside Denny and tried to breathe.

''HERRP!''

I, like, totally panicked. I threw the cover over the bird cage. The bird stopping hollering help. The bedroom was quiet. Too quiet. I uncovered the cage a little bit and peeked inside. The griffin glared back at me. "Bunkie?" I asked.

The griffin gnashed its beak. Denny shoved his sweaty little face next to mine. "T. E?"

"Aunt Matty?" I whispered.

The griffin cocked his head and chattered.

"It's not any of 'em." I sat back on my heels. "Or it's all of them, with the bird brain mixed up with the cat brain and the Aunt Matty brain."

"Do you want some oatmeal?" Denny asked the griffin in this high sweet voice, like this would fix everything.

I covered the cage up again. "We have to get it into Bunkie's cat carrier," I said. "And for gosh sakes, shut UP about this! One word to Mom or Dad and that important trip is like, down the tubes!"

Well, we messed around with the cat carrier for a bit, because the griffin didn't want to leave off guarding the pearl necklace, but as soon as I got that into the cat carrier, the griffin walked right in and settled down to guard like it'd been doing it all its life. Which it probably had, since it'd only been alive for about twenty-four hours. I'd just zipped the carrier shut when Mom came into Denny's bedroom and gave us both big hugs.

"I'm going to miss you guys."

I hugged her back, hard. "Sorry about the pink slip."

She smoothed my hair back. "I know you are, sweetie. We love you the way you are, pink slip and all," which made my eyes sting a little bit, and then Denny, the yahoo, started to sniffle, and pretty soon all three of us were standing there ready to bawl.

We all got packed up with the suitcases, the cat carrier, and the book bags, Althea Brinker included. We jammed into the elevator and went downstairs for the taxis. I didn't know what I was going to do if the darn griffin started hollering HEERRP! HEERP!, but except for bumping around in the cat carrier for a bit, it acted pretty normal.

Mom and Dad zoomed off in their taxi, waving and yelling, and the three of us got into another one and headed off for Penn Station to catch the Amtrak train for upstate New York.

Penn Station is kind of neat. It's like the biggest cave you ever saw, only made of marble, and when you walk in, the noise from all those people waiting for trains—and the poor people who come in from the streets to get warm when it snows out—is like being at the ocean. The trains are on all these different tracks underground, and you can hear them coming, like far-off rolling thunder. You wait by the turnstile with your ticket, and there's this huge *clackety, clackety, clackety* and a rush of warm wind. Then the train painted red, white, and blue for Amtrak comes to a screeching stop, and the windows in the cars, which have been snapping by like clothes on a line in a high wind, go slower, slower, slower, and then stop.

In each of the cars on the Amtrak is a place in the front where two seats face each other. If you get on early, you can get one, and it's great, because you can switch back and forth depending on whether you want to see the towns coming or going. We got the set in the third car. The griffin, which had been pretty quiet until we actually got on the train, started sort of an angry chirp and made a sound like "Ooooatmeaar!" which meant it'd been thinking about Denny's offer of oatmeal, and I hissed "Quiet!" and stuck the carrier in the overhead bin above my seat so I could reach up and grab it quick if it started to do anything weird. Then I shoved the rest of the luggage in the overhead, sat in the window seat facing the rest of the car, and acted casual.

We got rolling, and in about ten minutes, it seemed, we were clackety-clack clacking out of New York and into the countryside. After a while this Althea Brinker says, "Natalie?"

"Uh-huh."

"I'm sorry about that business with the unsatisfactory report. I thought your folks knew all about it."

This was okay. Maybe she was going to be all right after all.

Althea cocked her head. "Do you hear something?"

"No."

"It sounds like a bird."

It was the griffin, of course, muttering to itself up in the cat carrier on the top shelf, muttering what sounded like "oooaatmear, oatMEAR, OAT MEAR!"

"It's just Bunkie, settling in. She likes to go places in the cat carrier, but she always grumbles some."

"It doesn't sound like a cat."

"Well, it is a cat, and T. E., too."

"Your mom and dad said you don't usually take Denny's parakeet."

This was not okay. I couldn't afford to have this person being nosy. "We take T. E. down to the Silver Feather Deli when we go away. Old Mrs. Feather likes birds." This was the exact and literal truth. "We just didn't take T. E. down there this time." I didn't think that my fib quota counted with a fink tutor. The griffin shut up, thank goodness, and

Althea shrugged a little. Then she pulled out a map from her knapsack.

"Seventh grade is when you study New York State in geography," she said. "And we're going to one of the most interesting parts. Do you know much about the Finger Lakes area?"

Jeez, no, we just spend every summer there, for Pete's sake.

"Let me show you why it's called the Finger Lakes." She spread the map out on her knee, and I looked, to be polite. "You see how each of these five lakes—Canandaigua, Keuka, Skaneateles, Cayuga, and Seneca, form five fingers. We're going to Cayuga, right? That's where your uncle Bart's horse farm is. It's down here, close to the palm of the hand."

I stared at her. The spell! The spell had talked about the Palm of the Hand! I said, "What?" then cleared my throat and said louder, "What?"

"The palm is right here. Chimney Bluffs, on Lake Ontario."

I was just dying to get to the clue Mr. Feather had given me.

I had it memorized, of course. If I closed my eyes, I could see Mr. Feather's thin straight-up handwriting as clear as clear:

The Manitou's spirit will leave its earthly body when it descends the Chimney to guard the Treasure at the Heart of the World in the Palm of the Hand.

Absolutely awesome. We were headed straight to the place where I might be able to get my good old cat back after all. And Aunt Matty, of course. Chimney. It had to be Chimney Bluffs. Right in the Palm of the Hand. For a second, just a second, I wished I could trust this Althea with the secret of the griffin. What with all this education she was supposed to have, she might know something.

I remembered the pink slip. She'd probably call the cops or something.

"Could I see that map a second, Althea?"

"Sure." She smiled: student taking an interest. I wanted to smack her right in the ear. Instead, I peered at the map.

"There's ten lakes," I said. "It doesn't really form a human hand."

"Well, no, geographically speaking, that's true. But the smaller lakes aren't counted as one of the five Finger Lakes."

"How far is Chimney Bluffs from Uncle Bart's farm?"

"You measure that by looking at the scale, here." She pointed. "See? It's about and inch and a half for each ten miles. Hang on, I've got a ruler and you can figure it out yourself." She dug in that knapsack, which seemed to have everything but the kitchen sink, and produced a six-inch plastic ruler. I thanked her, and measured. Two inches or so. If an inch and a half was ten miles, then a half inch would be three and a third miles, so it was just under fourteen miles to the "chimney."

Which was a good day's ride on a horse.

"The Finger Lakes region was first settled by the Huron, Onondaga, and Seneca Indian tribes," said Althea. "Although, of course, since the white man moved in three hundred years ago, there hasn't been much left of the Indian culture."

Was I rolling or what? I had this, like, totally inspired

idea. "What about this Treasure at the Heart of the World?" I asked, very casual.

"Well, yes. Religion-wise, that's part of the lost Indian lore. A true anthropological tragedy. Most of the Huron and Seneca Indians traditions are gone."

"There is too Indians," said Denny, who had wakened up. "John's an Indian. He's not three hundred years old, is he, Natalie?"

"He's old, but nobody's that old. He's maybe forty or something."

"Who's John?" asked Althea.

"John Ironheels," I said. "He's the barn manager for my uncle. What he doesn't know about horses, nobody knows. Do you like to ride?"

"Well, I do, but I haven't ridden for a long time. I'd like to learn, though, again." She smiled. "Maybe you guys can teach me."

"I'll teach you," said Denny. "I'll teach you to ride Scooter." Now, this was typical Denny. I mean, Scooter was the rowdiest horse Uncle Bart had. A killer. Top riders had trouble with Scooter.

"Scooter," said Althea. "I'll remember that."

I grinned and decided not to say one little word.

The ride up to Uncle Bart's takes hours, mainly because the train stops for a while in each of the big cities it passes through. Albany is kind of cool because it's the state capital, although it set Althea off on another round of geography lessons. When we got through Albany to Seneca Falls, she told me that New York was the biggest dairy state in the United States, that New York was the second biggest apple grower, and that the shores of Lake Ontario were ideal for such fruits as cherries, peaches, and tomatoes. Did I know, she asked, that tomatoes are fruit?

I didn't know and I didn't care, but all this talk about food was making me hungry. I mentioned it, so we went into the dining car to eat some lunch in the late afternoon. It's neat to eat in the dining car of a train. Some of the trains don't have them, but this one did, and each of the tables had a white linen tablecloth on it, roses in the middle of the table with the salt and pepper shakers on each side, and heavy silverware. Denny chose a hamburger and fries, like he always does, and I got the spaghetti. Althea got the spaghetti, too, because she was trying to make up to me for being a fink, but it wasn't going to work. We ate and went back to our seats, Denny carrying part of his hamburger for later.

"Tell me about your uncle Bart," she said as we sat down.

I shrugged. "He's my mother's brother. A lot younger than Mom, I guess."

"Does your mother have any other brothers or sisters?"

The griffin let out this big SQUACK! I jumped about a foot.

"She used to," said Denny. "Aunt Matty. But she's dead."

The griffin started this thrashing around. I grabbed Denny's hamburger, jumped up, and stuffed it into the cat carrier.

"That parakeet sounds sick," said Althea. "And you've got your cat in there, too, Natalie? I think we should take a look."

"Aunt Matty got eaten up," said Denny. "Dead as a doornail."

Althea blinked. "Eaten by what?"

I kicked my little brother. "Denny's just making up stories, Althea. And Aunt Matty's just fine." I raised my voice so that stupid griffin could hear. "She doesn't get enough food, Mom says, and she gets really thin when she doesn't get enough food, she practically starves unless somebody helps her to eat—" I broke off. Althea looked at me like I'd lost my marbles. At least the griffin shut up. "Well," I said like a true feeb, "do you want to know about the horse farm?"

Althea opened her mouth like she was going to say something, shook her head, then said, "How many horses are there?"

I thought a minute. "Twenty, most times. Uncle Bart's a dressage trainer. Do you know what that is?"

"Sort of like horse ballet?"

She wasn't as dumb as all that, after all. "Kind of. He trains people and horses to ride in these special movements. There's four levels, like school. The kindergartners learn how to walk, trot, and canter very smoothly, to put their hooves in very particular ways. And then they get better and better at that until finally at fourth level, they're doing leaps and spins and pirouettes with a rider on their back."

"Can you do that?"

"Some of it," I said. "Uncle Bart gives me lessons every summer. But mostly I like to ride out camping." I looked at her. If I was going to go fourteen miles to Chimney Bluffs on a horse, carrying the griffin, I sure didn't want this tutor along. "Uncle Bart will probably give you lessons, too. There's a lot to learn before you can take a ride to go out—say, fourteen miles on a camping trip."

"This Scooter Denny mentioned. Is he a dressage horse, or a horse that likes to go camping? What are his talents?"

"Um. It's a she. A mare. Scooter's got lots of talents. All kinds of talents. Uncle Bart calls her a challenge."

"Then I'm really looking forward to it. I like a challenge. Well. I'm going to read a bit, now. You guys have anything to do?"

"We'll be fine. Go ahead."

She pulled a book out of her knapsack. I sat back, and mostly because I'd had all kinds of major shocks for the day, I was tired, so I fell asleep.

I woke up to Althea gently shaking my shoulder. The train had stopped. We were there. Denny was so fast asleep he didn't wake up at all, so Althea carried him, and her knapsack and his backpack, and I carried my stuff and the griffin. The griffin rustled in its cat carrier, and I whispered to it to shush if it wanted to eat again in this life. We got off the train. There was Uncle Bart, John Ironheels, and the dog Brandy, who sniffed at the cat carrier like it was a box of dog treats. I was so glad to see them all, I couldn't believe it!

Then we were in Uncle Bart's van, headed toward Cayuga Lake.

The griffin didn't make a sound as we got closer and closer to the Palm of the Hand.

BEFORE I WENT TO SLEEP THAT NIGHT, I'D FIGURED I'D get up before anyone else, sneak the griffin into the hay barn, and then find John Ironheels and learn how to get the griffin to the Palm of the Hand. I didn't explain any of this to Denny. I was still feeling weird about him, like he maybe wasn't the same little brother I'd always thought. Besides, he never even woke up when Uncle Bart stuck him into bed, and I didn't have time.

And of course, when I went into Denny's room the next morning, my bratty little brother and the griffin were gone.

Our bedrooms at Uncle Bart's are right next to each other, just off the top of the stairs in the old farmhouse. I've got the bedroom on the east side of the house, and when the sun slammed into my eyes and woke me up, I jumped into my jeans and zipped into Denny's room. Work on a horse farm starts early; by the time the sun is high enough to shine into my window, everybody's in the barn and morning feed is practically over. So I knew I was too late, but I went into Denny's room anyway. His stuff was scattered all over the floor, as usual. I tripped over his sneakers, as usual, and I threw his stuff all around, but the cat carrier with the griffin in it wasn't there. Neither was Denny.

I stared out Denny's window at the buildings below, wondering where a six-year-old kid would hide a griffin. And what he was doing with it.

Uncle Bart's place is called Stillmeadow Farms. The buildings are set in the shape of a big U. They are all connected so that in wintertime, you can get around the whole place without having to go outside in a blizzard. The Big Barn, which is the bottom of the U, has stalls for twenty horses. Even Denny would know that the griffin would make the horses freak, so I could be pretty sure he wouldn't take it there. One side of the U is a gigantic indoor riding arena; riding lessons start pretty early, and there'd be people around, so Denny wouldn't have taken it there, either.

The middle of the U is a huge open area paved with brick called the Yard. I stared at the Yard. Things looked normal. I could see Uncle Bart taking a couple of horses across to the fenced paddocks. John Ironheels was there, too, sticking a bunch of packed saddlebags into the pickup truck. He got in and drove off, which meant that'd be one thing I'd have to wait to do.

Brandy the dog was running around sniffing at stuff like she always does.

Suddenly Brandy went stiff, like somebody had called her, then she ran off and disappeared behind the hay barn.

Brandy really likes Denny. I thought about the hay barn for a second. The other side of the U is called the hay barn, but it contains Uncle Bart's office, the feed bins, the hay storage, and a totally cool place called the tack room, which holds all the saddles and bridles and horse stuff. The tack room smells absolutely neat, like clean horses and soft leather. The office and the tack room are usually pretty busy, but nobody's allowed to hang around the place where the hay and oats are stored.

I squinted at what I could see of the hay barn. No sign of Denny, the bozo. Or the griffin, which had to be getting pretty hungry by now, only having had part of a hamburger yesterday. I remembered how it'd practically smacked through that plate-glass window after a poor little pigeon.

Could it have eaten Denny? a little part of my mind whispered.

"Oh, ha!" I said, like how ridiculous, but the "ha" sounded nervous, even to me. Not that there was anybody there to hear how nervous I was.

I rushed through brushing my teeth and that stuff and ran downstairs to the kitchen: empty, except for a little bit of orange juice left in a pitcher on the table and a couple of plates with toast crumbs on them.

I'd been pretty sleepy myself last night, but I remembered that Uncle Bart gave Althea Brinker the little room off the kitchen for a bedroom. I peered in there, and naturally it was, like, incredibly neat, with the bed made and all her stuff put away already. Just like Denny, she wasn't there, either.

I heard this *thump-whack* from outside, jumped about a foot, and turned around faster than Mr. Feather's second nephew, who teaches karate. Which I was beginning to wish I'd learned. There was this *whack-whack-whack* from the back door and then a bark-WHUFF!

"Brandy," I said, that good old dog. I went to the back door to let her in. Brandy's a golden retriever, which is practically the best dog there is. She's got this beautiful round head and great body language when she sees you. It's like "how are you—how are you—how ARE you!" with her tail going faster than the Amtrak. Then her tongue hangs out in a big grin. Now, this dog had seemed normal last night when we got here. But she seemed different this morning. I watched her a second through the screen door.

For one thing, she looked at me. I mean, really *looked* at me, like another person does. Dogs don't usually look at you straight on.

For another, she sat down, reached up with one paw, stuck it through the latch handle, and pulled it open.

Brandy's a smart dog, but I'd never seen her do that before. I figured she wanted to come in and have some breakfast, so I waited, expecting her to come in jumping all over the place, but she backed up, barked again, and whirled toward the hay buildings.

"Come on, girl. I'll give you some dog food."

Brandy pointed her nose to the sky and yipped. Then she ran a little way toward the hay barn again.

"You want me to follow you, girl?"

Brandy yipped again.

I took a big guess. "Do you know where Denny is?"

Brandy yipped twice.

Now, two days ago, before my little brother had turned my aunt into a griffin, I would have said that talking to a dog like Brandy was strictly for people with propellers for brains. And I would have said that those propellers were moving pretty fast if a person thought that the dog talked back.

But I swear that dog barked, "Yep! Yep!" I looked
around to make sure nobody could see me talking to a dog
(and getting answers, for Pete's sake), and followed Brandy
around the back of the Big Barn to the hay barn. Brandy
bounced ahead like a piece of gold rubber and stopped at
the big wood door that slides open when hay is delivered
in the trucks. It was partly closed now. Brandy pranced up
to it, sat down, and stuck her head around the edge to look
into the barn and gave a bark that had a "they're here"
feel to it.

This dog was NOT behaving like a dog, if you get my
meaning. The back of my neck felt funny. "Denny?" I
said, in a real low voice.

I tiptoed to the door. Brandy walked inside, then turned
and looked at me, like "come in!" It was dark inside with
that dry grassy smell that hay barns get, like sunshine in a
bottle. I could see a stack of hay bales, and beyond them
a greeny glow.

I'd seen that greeny light before. In our kitchen, in New
York. When this whole magic started.

"Denny!" I whispered.

The light winked out.

There was a long silence. My heart was pounding like
you wouldn't believe. What was Denny *doing*?

If it *was* Denny in there.

"Denny!" I said, louder than I meant to.

"What?" Denny's voice sounded normal, which is to
say, totally bratty. I saw Brandy's tail wave harder and
harder, and then Denny's scruffy head came up over the
hay bales. He stuck the cat carrier on the top bale and
climbed up next to it. I shoved the wooden door open to
let in some light and went inside.

"Are you all right?"

He looked at me. "Huh?"

"I said are you okay? Not that I'm worried or anything," I said in this real sarcastic way. "I mean, you only snuck out of the house and scared me half to death." I waited a second, to calm down, then said in a more normal voice, "Is *it* in there?"

Denny shook the cat carrier.

"Herp me, *Herp me,* HERP ME!" said the griffin in this really annoyed way.

"What have you been doing?" I whispered angrily. "I can't believe that you took *it* out here without asking me. Did you feed it? Has anybody seen it?"

"Nope."

"Nope you haven't fed it or nope nobody's seen it."

Why do little kids do anything! Denny shoved the cat carrier at Brandy, who sniffed it, her tail wagging. "Aaagh!" shrieked the griffin.

"Denny!" I grabbed the cat carrier. That's all I needed, that Aunt Matty and my cat end up as breakfast for this dog. I gave Denny a really hard look. He was wearing yesterday's T-shirt, which was usual when Mom wasn't around to make him change it, and no socks. There were toast crumbs on his jacket and egg stains from breakfast on the side of his mouth. All in all, he looked pretty normal. I shook my head. I felt like flies were buzzing in my brain. Maybe I'd just imagined it—the magic green light, the dog talking to me. Things were weird enough without my imagination making them even weirder.

"Okay," said Denny, although *I* hadn't said a thing. It was like somebody else had, who wasn't there. He set the cat carrier on a hay bale and unzipped it.

"Denny! Don't! What if It escapes! What if—" I grabbed him and shoved him behind me.

The griffin stalked out, fluttered its wings a little bit, and cocked its head to one side and then the other. It looked at Brandy and snapped its beak twice, just like Aunt Matty on the phone to her guys at her office. Brandy whined, lay down, and put her paws over her head.

"There's LOTS of rats in here," said Denny to the griffin. "Uncle Bart'll be really happy if you catch 'em. We'll be back. Come on, Brandy."

And he marched out of the barn, the dog following. The griffin flew to the top of a bigger pile of hay and peered around the darkness, looking for rats, I guess. I stood there like a dodo for about a minute and a half, and then went after him.

"Denny!" I grabbed him by the T-shirt. "You can't just leave it in there!"

"Ike wanted breakfast," said Denny. "She'll stay in the barn and catch breakfast herself."

"Ike?" I said "Ike?"

There was a squawk, a sound of a bird flying, and an eep!

Denny shot his fist in the air. "Victo-ree! Ike, one. Rats, zero!"

I looked back over my shoulder, shuddered, and pulled the wooden door shut.

"Denny, listen. You've got to help me get that *thing* back in the cat carrier. Okay? If Althea or Uncle Bart see it we're in trouble."

"Nope! You leave Ike alone!" Denny took off like a redheaded beach ball around the side of the barn to the brick yard, with me and Brandy chasing him. I caught up with him, grabbed him by the T-shirt again, and held him up in front of me. "Its name is Ike?" Denny squirmed. I shook him. "Denny, if you can talk to it, maybe it can tell us how to get Aunt Matty back. And T. E. Don't you want T. E. back?"

"Lemme GO!"

Denny is a good wriggler, I'll give him that. I held on pretty tight and we both got a little sweaty, but I was pretty close to mashing the truth out of him when this girl came around the corner of the barn leading a horse and went, "Ick!" with this incredibly stuck-up expression on her face. And then: "What a filthy little boy!"

A boy leading another horse practically bumped right into her. A part of me noticed that he was even cuter than Brian Kurlander. A bigger part of me was so mad at this stuck-up girl that I sort of forgot he was there. I mean, what kind of a person calls somebody's little brother filthy when she doesn't even know you?

I let Denny go. This girl had perfect brown hair, perfectly cut. She wore little gold earrings in both ears. Plus, she was perfectly dressed in these perfect tan breeches and shiny black riding boots. Just . . . perfect.

Definitely a snot.

"It's just the barn help, Brett," said the boy behind her. "Shouldn't you be cleaning out the manure in the horse stalls, you two? And would you mind doing it now? You're in our way."

Ho. Another snot.

"Jeff's right. Why don't you just get back to work?" This girl walked right past me, leading her horse by the reins, so that I had to jump out of the way or get stepped on. The horse kind of rolled its eyes at me, like an apology, then the boy, who I decided must be this Brett's brother because they looked totally perfect in the same way, brought his horse by, too, and Denny did get stepped on, by the boy, not the horse. Horses are usually too cool to step on you, unless it's a mistake.

"Hey!" said Denny, and punched this kid Jeff.

Now, this kid had to be fifteen, at least, and he wasn't huge or anything, but he smacked my little brother right back, which of course, is a lot worse than his snotty sister calling Denny filthy, so I marched right over, shoved this kid out of the way, and said "Cut it OUT!" and Denny shrieked, "Banzai!" or something, and Jeff smacked Denny in the mouth! Denny bit back, of course.

I grabbed Denny and Uncle Bart came running up and said, "Hold on!" in a way that made everybody step back a few feet and just breathe instead of fighting.

"The little brat bit me!" Jeff howled. He waved his hand in the air like it'd been cut off at the wrist, or something. I didn't know what *his* problem was. There was only a little blood.

"Natalie," said Uncle Bart. "What's going on here?"

Now, Uncle Bart is totally cool, so I said, perfectly un-flapped, "This *person* stepped on Denny, Denny smacked the person back, and then he hit Denny in *the mouth*." Expecting that Uncle Bart would run this boy off the farm.

But to my absolute eternal astonishment, Uncle Bart calmly said, "Go up to the farmhouse, Denny. And Jeff? Come with me to the tack room. I'll bandage this up for you. Sorry about this, Brett."

Sorry! Sorry that this huge fifteen-year-old creep hit my brother?

And Uncle Bart marched of with this Jeff, even holding

his horse for him, and Denny ran off to the house, howling. The girl, Brett, made a satisfied noise like, "Hm!" and said, "You should teach that little boy better manners," then jerked her horse around and got up into the saddle.

There's a term my Scottish grandmother used: *gob-smacked*. It means, like, absolutely amazed. Stunned. Well, I was gob-smacked, that's for sure. Had everyone around here gone crazy?

The horrible Brett jerked on her horse's mouth and made it rear a little bit, then galloped off to the wooded trail behind the pastures, which left Brandy and me standing there, gob-smacked.

"What do you think, girl?"

Brandy just looked at me, wagged her tail, then sat down and scratched behind her ear just like any dog you'd meet any day of the week.

"I tell you what I think. I think this griffin is messing up more than my cat, the parakeet, and Aunt Matty. And Denny's the one who knows what's going on."

So Brandy and I marched back to the kitchen and found Denny eating all the toaster pastries.

"Quit that," I said coming into the kitchen. "You should eat some fruit or yogurt or something." I was starved, so I stuck a couple of strawberry pastries in the toaster and sat down across from him at the kitchen table.

"All right, Denny, spill it."

Denny's feet are too short to reach the floor in regular-sized chairs. He grinned, thumped his feet against the chair leg, rolled his eyes up to the ceiling, and opened his mouth so I could see big chunks of chewed blueberry toaster pastry. He drooled the mess down the front of his T-shirt. It was disgusting.

"Stop that."

"You said spill it."

"You know what I mean. What did that griffin tell you?!"

Bang! Bang! Bang! went Denny's feet. "You know those two kids?"

I stuck my hands in my hair. I wanted to scream. "Don't change the subject, Denny. We've got more important things to worry about than those guys. Just . . ." I made myself very, very calm. All that happens when you holler at Denny is that he gets more stubborn. "Just tell me what's going on with the griffin. You called her Ike?" I smiled at him, a big grin that even an six-year-old could tell was fake.

Denny swallowed and burped on purpose. "The big kid is Jeffrey, Brett's brother. Their dad owns this place. Mr. Loomis."

This was so ridiculous I stopped thinking about Aunt Matty for a minute. "Uncle Bart owns this place."

Brandy barked twice.

"Huh?" said Denny to the dog.

Brandy barked again.

"Mr. Loomis *almost* owns this place," said Denny, like Brandy had made him change what he was saying. "Mr. Loomis owns the more-gage."

"The mortgage? You mean the bank loan on the farm?"

Brandy barked, "Yep."

Jeez!

"And Mr. Loomis can make Uncle Bart pay this more-gage anytime he wants."

I said, very carefully, "Did Brandy tell you that?"

Denny nodded, like this happened every day of the week, that dogs talked to him.

I leaned over and looked at Brandy, who was lying under

the table at Denny's feet, opened my mouth, and couldn't think of a thing to say to this dog. Or to Denny. I straightened up again. What you have to do with six-year-olds, Mom always said, was take one thing at a time. And the most important thing right now was to get my cat back. And Aunt Matty, of course.

"So, the griffin's name is Ike?"

"Uh-huh."

"Is it a him or a her?"

Denny shrugged. "It's a griffin."

I didn't know why I'd asked this anyway. Why would a magical creature have to be anything like a human?

"Is—ah—Aunt Matty in the griffin anywhere? And Bunkie? Is Bunkie in the griffin anywhere?" I sneaked a look at Brandy again. If Denny could talk to Brandy because of the magic this griffin was making, maybe I could end up talking to my good old cat.

Denny did his rubber-lips act, which is making gross faces with his mouth. "Okay. It's like this. You know when you put sugar and flour and stuff in a cake. And you stick it in the oven and you get a cake, right? But you don't have flour or sugar or eggs, you have cake." He grinned. His teeth were blueberry-colored. And a six-year-old with blueberry-colored teeth was giving me chemistry lessons. I mean, I could hardly dissolve the griffin into Aunt Matty molecules and sort of reassemble them. Could I?

Denny slobbered down the rest of his blueberry pastry and I told him to go to the sink and wash up.

I dug into my jeans pocket and took out the spell.

The Manitou's spirit will leave its earthly body when it descends the Chimney to guard the Treasure at the Heart of the World in the Palm of the Hand.

I still hadn't figured out why old Mrs. Feather was calling the griffin a manitou, but at least I'd figured out one clue. According to the map of the Finger Lakes, the Palm of the Hand was right near Chimney Bluffs. And that was a two-hour ride from here on a good horse. And if I read this clue right, the griffin would leave Aunt Matty, Bunkie, and T. E. behind to go guard this Treasure at the Heart of the World, just like it'd jumped into the cat carrier to guard the pearl necklace back in Manhattan. Unless, like eggs and sugar and flour in a cake, the molecules wouldn't go back together.

It was too horrible. Magic wasn't supposed to make sense like chemistry did—was it?

So I'd figured out two clues. Which meant there were two left. To find out what kind of magic could unbake the cake. And to figure out what the Treasure at the Heart of the World was and get the griffin to guard it. Good old Althea said that treasure was part of Indian legend, and there was a terrific Indian right here at Stillmeadow Farms. John Ironheels. And as far as the magic was concerned, well, John could fix that, too. He was a shaman, a wise man of his tribe. The toaster popped up with my strawberry pastries. I poured myself the rest of the orange juice and bit into a pastry. I sat back with a sigh of relief. Things weren't nearly as bad as I'd thought when I'd gotten up that morning. As soon as I finished my breakfast, I'd go look for John, make Denny talk to the griffin, and we'd get this thing settled before anybody knew Aunt Matty was gone.

Brandy barked. A warning bark.

"Cool!" said Denny, at the kitchen window.

"Cool, what?" I asked, being unflapped and relaxed for the first time in two days.

"Cool, it's the cops!" Denny turned away from the sink. I jumped up and looked over his shoulder. It was the cops all right: a big black-and-white state trooper's car, with a uniformed guy in a cowboy hat getting out.

Uncle Bart and Althea came up to the car. All three of them talked. Uncle Bart looked at the kitchen window. He said something to Althea. She nodded and came trotting into the kitchen.

"Hey, guys," she said. "Did you both get some breakfast?" She didn't wait for an answer. Her red hair was kind of blown around, like she'd been sticking her hands into it or something. "Look. I don't want you to get upset, but Officer Schmidt would like to ask you some questions, okay? You don't need to be nervous or anything, but it's about your aunt Matty. She didn't turn up for her conference yesterday. Your mom's cleaning lady found her suitcase and her fur coat in Manhattan, Natalie. Under your bed."

CHAPTER

Five

WE FOLLOWED ALTHEA OUT TO THE CRUISER WHERE OF-
ficer Schmidt was standing with Uncle Bart. Officer
Schmidt was so big he sort of blotted out everything else.
I peered up at him with my best ''I'm clueless!'' expression. This works pretty well in homeroom when I don't
want to rat on Arnie Montgomery for throwing spitballs. It
didn't seem to work on this state trooper. He had piercing
blue eyes. He didn't smile.

''Natalie,'' said Uncle Bart, ''this is a friend of mine,
Ed Schmidt. We go back a long way. And Ed, this is my
niece Natalie Ross, and my nephew Denny.''

''You're sure this is okay with you, Bart?'' asked Officer
Schmidt. ''I mean the kids' folks aren't here and all.''

''Why, I think so,'' said Uncle Bart. ''They must have
been the last to see Matty before she disappeared. If she
has disappeared, Ed. You know Madeline and that company of hers. It's the first and last thing she thinks about.

If she'd found some unsuspecting pigeon, she'd jump right
on it without a thought to anyone else."

"Rats," said Denny. "Aunt Matty likes rats better."

I poked Denny to shut up. Officer Schmidt and Uncle
Bart went "ho-ho-ho" like Denny'd said something funny
instead of the literal truth. Althea didn't go "ho-ho-ho,"
though. She looked at Denny and then at me with a very
peculiar expression.

"I just want you kids to let me know a few things. Your
uncle's going to stand right here." He squatted down so
he didn't seem to be nine feet tall, only about eight. "And
don't be nervous, little lady."

Little lady? I gave this bozo a piercing look right back.

"That's a real gun?" Denny said.

"Yes, son, it is."

"Shoot anybody with it?"

"Yes, son, I have."

Jeez!

"Now, Natalie. When did you last see Ms. Carmichael?
We found a note that said she had to leave on business.
Did you overhear any phone calls? Did anyone come to the
apartment to see her?" He peered at me, his eyes keen.
"Did you write the note after she left? Most important, did
she tell you she'd be back in a few days herself?"

It was very, very quiet. It was so quiet, I could hear those
horses still in their stalls stamping around waiting to be let
out to pasture.

Now, maybe you've noticed. Once about every million
years—and it's usually when dumb Denny has gotten us
into a big pile of trouble—I've had to tell a couple of fibs.
I know I'm going to get it when the fib is found out, but I

figure that's the price I have to pay. I mean, a person can't just let her dorky little brother zoom right into total disaster, can she?

Besides, fibs are practically the truth. A person who leaves some of the parts of the truth out isn't a liar. Aunt Matty DID have to go away for a few days. While she was in the griffin's body. So the note I left wasn't a lie. Exactly. I'm *not* the sort of person who tells lies. Once in a million years a temporary fib is, like, necessary. But there was no way to answer Officer Schmidt's question with a fib. It looked like the whole truth would have to come out that very minute.

I sighed. They'd probably lock Denny up with a child psychologist for five hundred years. Me, they'd put in the reformatory. I wouldn't see Brian Kurlander until I was twenty-two.

Officer Schmidt straightened up slowly, like a huge building crane, waiting. I could tell the story for Denny. He wouldn't have to say a thing. I'd tell them *I* was the one who'd turned Aunt Matty into the griffin and leave Denny out of it altogether. I mean, Denny would make hash of any child psychologist living. I might just as well not have some poor innocent child psychologist on my con-science along with everything else.

My hands were sweaty. I wiped them on my jeans. Denny stuck his thumb in his mouth and put his other hand—all gooey with blueberry pastry—into mine and sighed this teeny little sigh.

"Well, sir," I said, "it all started at the Silver Feather Deli."

Then John-Henry-Holy-Jehoshaphat broke loose in the barn.

Actually, it wasn't the barn but the riding arena. There were shrieks, hollers, and surprised neighs from what sounded like a whole herd of horses. Then, there was a *ka-thump, ka-thump, CRASH!* Brandy took off like a furry rocket, with all of us running behind.

Uncle Bart got to the riding arena first. He dived in the middle of the mess. Brett Loomis was hanging on to the pommel of her saddle, one foot in the stirrup and the other hopping along the ground, trying to keep up as her horse trotted around and around the arena. Its eye was rolling so you could see the white part, which meant it was scared. Jeff's horse was galloping around the arena the other way from Brett's horse, the reins hanging loose. Every time the two horses passed each other, they sort of kicked out with their hind legs and Brett would scream this icky little scream.

I looked around for Jeff himself. The manure'd been scooped up from the arena in a pile by the far end, and Jeff's feet were waving out of the top of it where his good old horse had dumped him.

It was pretty hilarious.

Uncle Bart dashed after Brett's horse. Officer Schmidt went after Jeff's horse, caught it, and tied it to the rail on the far side of the arena. Althea went over to Jeff and gave him a hand out of the manure pile.

I heard a quiet *scraw* from overhead and looked up. The griffin crouched on the rafters over the middle of the arena, snaky dragon's tail curled around its claws. I made shooing motions with my hands. It crawled up out of sight, leaving a greeny-gold cloud behind it.

In the arena, Brett pitched a major hissy fit. Those perfect breeches were all over horse manure where she'd hopped through the pile near the back door. I wondered if she'd kicked her brother, or if he'd fallen in after she'd plowed through it. Her perfect hair was muddy, too. She was the sort of person who wears makeup to go riding, so eyelash goo was streaked all over her cheekbones. She looked gross.

There were advantages to having this griffin flying loose, I could see that right away.

Brett screamed that Uncle Bart was stupid for not teaching this horse to behave. Then she screamed that Uncle Bart was a slob because of the manure pile. Now, the manure pile was right where it's supposed to be. That's where the truck comes to get it every morning. Did she expect horses to use flush toilets or what? Then she blamed the horse for being a fool, stamped over, grabbed it by the reins, jerked its mouth, and yelled at it, too.

Jerking on a horse's mouth is not something you do at Uncle Bart's, even when your father owns the mortgage on the horse farm. Bridles have bits in them, and jerking on the bit hurts the horse. A lot. The person who stopped Brett from whacking on her horse was Officer Schmidt. I decided he could call me ''little lady'' anytime he wanted to.

''That's enough, missy,'' he said. He put his hands on Brett's shoulders, moved her away from the horse, took the reins, and handed them to Althea.

''My father's going to hear about this!'' Brett hollered. ''And he'll throw you all out of here, just like he did that stupid Indian!''

''John's fired?'' I blurted out. ''Oh, no!'' I mean, who was going to help me with figuring out this American Indian anthropology stuff!

Uncle Bart gave me a long look. ''Ed,'' he said. ''Maybe

we better wait until my sister and brother-in-law get here before you ask the kids any more questions.''

Officer Schmidt looked very disappointed. Me, I was relieved.

"Your call, Bart. I'll just run Brett and her brother home. And I'll do the explaining to Loomis, about the little accident in the manure pile.'' Officer Schmidt gave Brett a little shove toward the back door and jerked his head at Jeff to come along. Brett's face was the color of spaghetti sauce. Jeff's was, too. Nobody said anything until we heard the police cruiser leave the brick yard. Then nobody said anything for a while after that.

Uncle Bart sighed. His shoulders sagged. Althea patted Brett's horse, who had calmed down by now.

"What did Brett mean, that Mr. Loomis will throw you all out of here like he did the Indian?'' asked Althea. "Did she mean John Ironheels, your barn manager?''

Uncle Bart nodded.

"John's *fired*?'' I blurted out, again. Like, I couldn't believe this.

"I'm doing the best I can, Natalie. I know how close you all were. And God knows things are upset enough around here without adding this business about Matty to your worries. Look here.'' He crouched down and looked right in my face. "A place like this . . . the expenses. It's hard to keep up.''

"But you fired John?! How could you?''

"Mr. Loomis said I couldn't afford him. He was right.'' Uncle Bart's eyes were sad. He heard me, I guess, but he had stood up again and was looking at Althea. "I'm not like my sisters, Althea. Or my brother-in-law, either. I just don't seem to have a head for the business end of things.

It was either lose John or the farm itself. As it is, I don't know how long I'm going to be able to keep things running on my own.''

Somewhere overhead, the griffin growled. For once, I kept my big mouth shut. I was stunned. Shocked. Worse than gob-smacked. Uncle Bart without the horse farm?

''If Matty were here, I might have a chance. I was hoping she could advise me about refinancing—maybe finding a bank that wouldn't charge as much interest as Loomis is charging me . . . but, never mind.'' He straightened up. A kind of fake smile creased his face. ''This isn't your problem, Althea. Or yours either, Nat. Hey! How would you and Denny like to go riding? It's a beautiful morning out there. Why don't you two take Althea with you. Blow the cobwebs out of our brain. Forget all this.''

''Is there anything we can do to help you around here, Bart?'' Althea asked.

''No. No. To tell you the truth, I'd rather just handle things myself, this morning. I need some time to think.''

''I guess we could put the tutoring off for a while.'' Althea bent her head back and searched the rafters, her eyes narrow. ''I wanted to get some time alone with Natalie and Denny anyway. So, sure. I'd love to try riding.''

''All right. I'll leave you guys to it. Give her a nice quiet horse, Natalie. She hasn't ridden for a long time. I'll see you all around lunchtime.''

''I thought you didn't know how to ride at all,'' I said, after Uncle Bart had taken the Loomis horses out of the arena.

''I rode quite a bit when I was younger. But it's been a long long time.'' Althea smiled, and if I'd thought I could trust her, I would have liked the smile. It was, I don't know—sort of shy. Which is nice. A lot of people say they can ride when they really can't. Althea wouldn't be so bad if she didn't say things like "anthropologically speaking" all the time.

"From an equestrian standpoint, I'm a little nervous," Althea went on, "since it has been such a long time. And I'm really out of shape, so if we could just go for a short time, I could see how much I remember, and I won't get too stiff."

Now, the last thing I wanted was this bogus tutor hanging around all day while I tried to figure a way out of this mess, even if I was beginning to like her a little bit. I had to get Denny to talk to the griffin. And Denny and I had to get the spell to John Ironheels, to see if he knew what the heck the Treasure at the Heart of the World was, which Althea herself had said was Indian lore, and who would know about Indian lore better than an Indian? Plus, I sure didn't like the way Althea was looking from me to the roof where the griffin was supposed to be hiding, and then to Denny. She suspected something, or my name wasn't Natalie Carmichael Ross. Nope, I definitely didn't want Althea hanging around all day, asking questions.

"If you don't remember how to ride," said Denny, who'd been suspiciously quiet for ten whole minutes, "I'll teach you. I'll teach you on Scooter."

"Yeah," I said. "We'll teach you on Scooter."

Scooter. The rowdiest horse in the barn. All we had to do was find someplace soft for Althea's first ride. Like near the manure pile.

It was kind of fun, showing Althea where everything was, sort of like I was the tutor and she was the person that had to stand there and have somebody else be the boss.

And she was really interested, you could tell.

Stillmeadow Farms has three kinds of horses: the boarders, the show horses, and the lesson horses. Boarders are the same as renting an apartment or a condo. People who own horses but don't have a place to keep them rent stall space. Uncle Bart feeds them and keeps the stalls clean and turns the horses out every day to get fresh air and grass. The owner is supposed to come and brush them and ride them.

The show horses are just for Uncle Bart and the professional riders. They go all over the country to compete in shows. Uncle Bart's horses always win a lot of blue ribbons.

Then there are the lesson horses. These are horses Uncle Bart owns. He teaches people to ride on them. You learn to ride with *cues*. A cue is where you place your hands or feet or legs or backside. Cues tell the horse what to do. There are beginning-, intermediate-, and advanced-lesson horses, according to what kind of cues the rider and the horse know. A beginning horse would know how to walk, trot, and canter with the right cues. An advanced horse would know how to jump a lot of four-foot fences very smoothly, or do advanced movements like a pirouette. If you put a beginning rider on an advanced horse, the horse doesn't know what to do when it gets kicked and bumped in the wrong place. So for instance, if you accidentally stuck your toe behind the saddle at the wrong time, an advanced horse would think it was supposed to jump like over a truck or whatever.

Scooter was an advanced-lesson horse.

The other thing about horses is that they have personalities. Some are like Normie Hedrick at school, who looks

as nice as butter when you talk to him, but puts gross stuff
in your locker when you aren't looking, and sneaks chewed
gum into your hair if you bump into him accidentally in
the hall. Others are like my best friend, Nan, who does
everything right the first time.

Scooter and Normie Hedrick would have gotten along
just fine.

Scooter was out in the pasture with the other lesson
horses, so we took lead ropes and halters with us to go get
them. All of them were out there, chomping away at the
grass like anything, under the clear spring sky.

My special horse at Stillmeadow is a chestnut mare
named Mindy Blue. She's got a white blaze on her nose
and four white feet. Her coat is the color of a maple leaf
in October. She is absolutely, totally cool. Every year I
come back, I talk to her. She sticks her nose in my hair
and sniffs, and then she remembers who I am. Uncle Bart
says that horses remember differently from the way that
people do: by scent and by sound and by feel. So I make
sure to pet her in the same place, and say the same things,
and even use the same shampoo, so that I smell the way I
did before.

I know that Susie, the Shetland pony that Denny rides,
remembers who he is every year, too. When Denny comes
into the pasture to get her, hollering "Susieee!" that pony
takes off like a motorcycle. Uncle Bart says that's just the
way ponies are, and doesn't have to do with Denny at all.
Me, I think this pony is *smart* to run like heck from Cowboy Dennis.

While Denny was chasing Susie all over the pasture, I
pointed out Scooter to Althea.

"It's that buckskin mare, right there. The one with the creamy coat and the black mane and tail."

Scooter jerked her head up with a snort when Althea walked up to her, then bent her head to accept the halter and the lead rope. Nice as pie. Smooth as butter.

I caught Susie for Denny and we led the horses back to the barn to tack them up. Denny rides in a Western saddle, which has this big horn in front so he can grab on when he thinks nobody is looking. He's pretty good at tacking up all by himself, so I got out Mindy's English saddle and bridle and got her all ready.

Althea chose a dressage saddle, which is not all that easy to sit. I mean, if you get into trouble, there's nothing to grab onto. I didn't say a word. She chunked the saddle over Scooter, then went under the horse to grab the girth and pull it tight. *Snick!* Good ol' Scooter snaked her head around and tried to take a nip out of Althea's elbow. Althea jumped, but she didn't squeal.

"I kinda forgot to mention it," I said. "Scooter's kind of cinchy."

"Cinchy?"

"She doesn't like the girth or cinch, rather, tightened around her belly. Keep your elbow out when you tighten the girth. She'll run into it when she swings her head around and she won't bite."

"Hm. Is there anything else you 'kinda forgot' to tell me?"

"I'll tell you as soon as I remember," I promised.

Althea stuck her elbow out and tightened the girth, cinching it up pretty well. This didn't impress me. Practically everybody knows you have to make sure the saddle doesn't slip. Scooter rolled one brown eye at me, took a deep breath, and held it.

Althea slipped the bridle over Scooter's head and brought the bit up to the mare's mouth. Scooter clamped her mouth shut.

"She does that," I explained. "You have to stick your hand in her mouth. Horses don't like the taste of human flesh. She'll open up and you can stick the bit in."

"I seem to remember that horses don't have teeth on the sides of their mouths, do they?"

"Nope. Just in front."

Althea stuck her hand in the side of Scooter's mouth. Scooter'd been chomping grass all morning, and she had lots of good old horse spit. Althea's shirt was pretty green by the time the bit got in.

"I think we should try riding in the arena, first," I said. "Just to see how things go."

We led the horses out of the tack barn into the arena. Good old Scooter was taking little tiny breaths, keeping her belly full of air. Denny hopped on Susie and started tootling around and around the arena. I led Mindy Blue to the front of the manure pile, made her stand, and got the mounting block. I swung myself into the saddle, moved away from the mounting block, and Althea led Scooter up to it.

Althea looked at me. Frowned. Slipped her hand between Scooter's belly and the girth, then tightened it.

"Some horses," Althea explained with a suspicious sort of look, "take in a lot of air when you put the saddle on, so that the saddle will slip off when you mount. Were you going to remember to tell me that?"

"Now that you mention it," I said, "I was." I was starting to feel a little bit like a skunk. "Scooter's very sensitive. I remember that, now that I come to think of it. Be careful about your cues. You know, cues are when you ask the horse to do something with your hands and your heels.''

''Sensitive, huh?'' said Althea. ''O-*kay*. You do remember I haven't ridden for a long, long time. And people can get hurt on horses, if they aren't careful?''

I blushed. I could feel it. I was like, repenting.

''As a matter of fact, maybe you'd want to ride Mindy Blue, here. And let me handle Scooter. Actually, Althea, she's not really . . .''

But Althea ignored me and swung into the saddle. Scooter stood still for a second, thinking, Althea nudged her sides with both heels. Scooter jumped straight up in the air, landed right in the spot where she'd been standing, then bucked like a son of a gun.

Althea stayed on!

Scooter stopped bucking and thought a little more. Suddenly she tossed her head up and began to back across the arena about ninety miles a hour. Denny whooped and raced Susie out of the way. Scooter backed, backed, backed, and Althea stuck on, rising out of the saddle, both hands low on the reins, with a lot of rein loose over the pommel. Since horses' eyes are set on the sides of their heads, they can see around themselves in a big circle. Scooter knew when she was getting close to the arena wall on the far side. She spun sideways, ready to mash poor Althea into the wall. Althea was ready for her. She pulled the left rein short, pulling Scooter's head away from the wall with a smooth, firm tug. She smacked Scooter's rump with the loose reins, dug her heels into Scooter's sides, and pushed the mare forward.

I was watching, holding my breath. I'm telling you, this

horse looked very surprised. Scooter made sort of a hiccup, shook her head, then put her ears forward and started to "listen." You know that a horse is "listening" to you when its head is down, its hindquarters are collected under its belly, and it's riding nice and smoothly.

By this time Denny had trotted Susie over to me, and we were sitting side by side on our horses, watching Althea work the mare. She moved Scooter into a smooth canter, working her in figure eights around and around the arena. Then she flexed her down to a trot, then a walk, and finally pulled her up in the center of the ring. Scooter arched her neck, snorted, then turned her head and nudged Althea's boot.

Althea put her into walk, so smoothly that I couldn't see the cue, and walked right up to us and stopped.

Mindy Blue put her ears forward and made a chuffing sound. Scooter chuffed back. Everybody sat very quietly for a minute.

"I'm really sorry," I said, finally.

"If I hadn't known how to ride . . ." said Althea.

"I really thought she'd just dump you. She always does that with people the first time out. That jump and buck. Practically everybody falls off right away."

"And the manure pile's nice and soft," Althea agreed.

"That's no excuse," I said. "You could have been hurt. And it would have been my fault. I didn't think. And I'm really sorry." I looked at my boots, embarrassed.

"Hey," said Althea. She reached over and patted my arm. "Here. It's okay. Most people would have quit when she tried to bite. And you did warn me, Natalie, just before I got on. So you didn't really mean to hurt me."

I rubbed my nose so she wouldn't see how embarrassed

I really was. "I'll never do anything like this ever again."

"Well—maybe that awful Brett could be encouraged to ride this mare. . . ." said Althea. "Just kidding. We've all learned a lesson here, I think."

"I just . . . I've had a lot on my mind."

This sounded lame, even to me, and *I* was the one making the excuse.

"Well, I know you have," said Althea. She looked up at the arena roof, like she had before. "I've been wanting to talk to you about the lizard in the cat carrier since yesterday."

CHAPTER

six

ALTHEA'D KNOWN ABOUT THE GRIFFIN ALL ALONG!

I was totally gob-smacked, again. Twice in one morning. I couldn't believe how the stuff I had to worry about was piling up: how could a manitou be a griffin, like Mrs. Feather's spell said? How could I get Ike to the Palm of the Hand? What was I supposed to do when I got Ike there?

Worst of all: how come Denny could all of a sudden talk to animals?

So for Pete's sake, now *Althea* knew about Ike!

While I was trying to put all this crazy stuff into some kind of order, Althea said, "You could have said something about the lizard in the cat carrier before, you know." She adjusted her glasses with one slim hand. "But I guess you thought I'd blow you in, after I'd told your parents about the geography grade. I haven't handled this well, psychologically speaking. I'm sorry about that. I could have checked with you first, to see how you were handling the course work. Then we could have talked to your folks to-

73

gether. But I hadn't met you before, Natalie. And I was anxious to impress your folks that I was going to do a good job. So you got caught looking like a slacker. And you aren't, of course. Far from it. I apologize. And, I think you've handled the last couple of days with a lot of guts.''

This made me smile. I reached down and patted Mindy Blue's sleek neck so Althea wouldn't see me grinning and think I was smug or anything. ''I guess I sort of lost my cool myself,'' I said. Mindy's mane was ruffled in the middle and I smoothed it out. ''So you know about the griffin. That's kind of a relief. We didn't mean to make it. It just . . . happened.''

''It was Aunt Matty's fault,'' said Denny. ''She did it. She was going to make us eat T. E. for dinner. So I fixed her.'' He smacked his lips in satisfaction.

Me? I got goose bumps. How much did Denny know about the spell old Mrs. Feather had given him, anyway?

''Fixed her?'' Althea cleared her throat a couple of times. ''You fixed your aunt Matty?''

Denny did his Superhero imitation, plowing his fist through the air like Arnold Schwarzenegger. ''KaPOW right in the kisser!''

''Denny! He didn't *mean* to do it,'' I explained. ''It was an accident. But I had to help him fix it, so I wrote that note that Aunt Matty'd gone away.''

''An accident,'' said Althea, kind of faint, like. ''So. What did he use . . . I mean how did he . . . ?'' Althea adjusted her glasses. Her hands were shaking. That business with rowdy old Scooter must have shaken her up more than I thought. ''Is the—what did you call it, griffin?—here right now?''

I scanned the rafters doubtfully. ''I don't think it's

around. That's what scared Brett and Jeff's horses a while ago. I think Mindy Blue and Scooter would be jumping around if it were in the arena.''

"How did it—um—get here, exactly?"

"In the cat carrier," said Denny, who is what they call literal-minded. This is the opposite of having an imagination, and Dad always said us kids drive him nuts in two different directions because of it. Denny with too little of an imagination. Me with too much.

"I know how it got *here*. I meant where did the griffin itself come from?" She rubbed her forehead with both hands. "A Gila monster, maybe? From the Bronx Zoo? But even you couldn't have broken into the Bronx Zoo, Natalie. And why would you call it a griffin when there's no such thing? I mean—well, psychologically speaking, it makes sense, I guess."

I'm glad it made sense to *her*. It still didn't make sense to me. "Where did Ike come from? That's a long story," I said in a cautious way. I wasn't sure how Althea was going to feel about magic, even though we had a pretty good example of it in the griffin itself. People could find all kinds of scientific excuses for perfectly good mysterious stuff. "It was old Mrs. Feather, actually, who gave Denny the talcum powder to make the griffin. She must be a magician, or something."

"This Mrs. Feather gave a six-year-old boy talcum powder to make a griffin?"

When she put it like that, old Mrs. Feather didn't sound very—what would Dad call it?—responsible.

"Well, you know magicians," I said. This sounded pretty lame to me, so I added, "Old Mrs. Feather *likes* Denny, though. I'm sure she had no idea we'd get into all this trouble.'' I turned around in the saddle and glared at Denny. "I'll bet you messed the spell up, Dennis Ross."

Denny scowled back at me. "I did not!"

"Well, you must have. I'll bet this was a temporary spell and you forgot part of it."

"You're missing my point," said Althea, with this "let me explain this VERY carefully" tone of voice. "I was speaking physically. Did the griffin come from a zoo? Did Mrs. Feather give it to you? Did she find it somewhere? Did she help you dispose of Aunt Matty's bod—I mean, you *must* have had an adult help you do this." She muttered something like "mittagating circumstances."

"A zoo?" said Denny, getting back to the point like he does.

"Well—that's where something like that would belong, wouldn't it?"

"You've seen it, you said," I said. I mean, that griffin looked just like a griffin to me.

"A zoo," said Denny. "You'd put Ike in a zoo?"

"Shut up, Denny," I said. "Althea, has anyone *else* seen the griffin?"

"Oh, no! No. No, No! That's a mercy, isn't it? I went into Denny's room to check on him last night while he was asleep. It was grumbling in the cat carrier, so I zipped the carrier open and took a look. I wasn't sure what you guys had in there, but I wasn't prepared for that! Is it something you were going to dissect in biology class, maybe? Is that where it came from? A Kokomanthu lizard?"

"Di-sek?" said Denny. He grabbed my arm. "What's di-sek?"

I shook Denny's hand off. "Leave me alone for one

whole minute, can't you? Althea, when you saw *it*, did you know what it was?''

"You said it was a griffin, didn't you?''

"DiSEK! That means cut it UP!'' Denny screeched.

"Denny! Shut up for two seconds!''

"Cut her up?'' Althea said. I hadn't paid much attention before, but Althea was a pretty pale person. Althea repeated. "You couldn't have . . . cut Aunt Matty up!

"I've seen pictures of griffins, of course,'' she said real fast. "I'm an anthropologist, or I will be when I finish my degree. You believe it's a griffin. Right. It's a griffin.''

"Do you—hum-hum!'' I cleared my throat, which seemed to have gotten stuck. "Do you know *who* this griffin is?''

"I know that in ancient mythology, a griffin's a dragon, an eagle, and a lion. I know that cat carrier should have held your cat Bunkie and Denny's parakeet. From what I've heard of your aunt Matty . . . well, they called her the Dragon of Wall Street, didn't they? And of course, with your aunt Matty's, ah, disappearance, I can see where the denial kicks in.''

What?

"So! It's not too hard to figure out where the third part was supposed to come from. I understand, Natalie. Believe me, everyone will understand what you think has happened.''

Where the griffin was *supposed* to come from? What I *think* happened?

I squinted at Althea, who said to herself, "The psychological ramifications are fascinating. Fascinating. And one must be objective in the pursuit of the truth. It's not too late to switch majors. Clinical psychology is a very rewarding field. And the paper I could write! I shall reserve judgment until I know more."

What the heck!

Then she said with this bright look, "So, tell me more about this. Tell me all. You said old Mrs. Feather gave Denny some talcum powder and a magic spell. You're claiming Denny made the griffin?"

"Denny did make the griffin. I'm the one trying to unmake it."

"I see. So, since then, you've been trying to figure out a way to get the griffin—well, dematerialized, so to speak." She put her hand out to pat me again, I guess, then drew it back. Tutors are just plain weird. Plus, I wasn't sure about this word *dematerialized,* but if it meant unbaking the cake, like Denny said, Althea had the right idea.

"Yes! And I think the key's in the magic," I said. "Do you believe in magic?"

"I'm an anthropologist. I reserve judgment on magic." She looked at me in the same way Officer Schmidt had. "Tell me about this magic."

I looked back at her pretty hard, my doubts all buzzing around again. Maybe it'd be better if Denny explained the magic to her. It always seemed to me that people gave six-year-olds like Denny a lot of slack. And besides, he was the one who had screwed up the spell in the first place. "Denny, Ike's been in your room, and you've been talking to *it,*" I said without looking around.

"Oh, it talks, too?"

I was losing patience, here. "It doesn't talk to me, really. It talks more to Denny." *Why* Ike told Denny all this stuff and not me was something I couldn't think about just yet. "I mean, he says the darned thing's named Ike. How could a six-year-old make up a name like Ike?'' Actually, a six-year-old like Denny is capable of a lot more than just that, so I got off the subject. "Tell Althea what happened, Denny."

No answer.

"Denny!"

Still no answer. I looked down at my right side, where Denny and his short little pony had been just two minutes ago and weren't now. Denny and Susie the Shetland had disappeared.

"Dang! DENNY!"

"You don't suppose . . ." Althea trailed off.

"What?"

"That the griffin's dangerous or anything. I mean. It couldn't have carried him off, it's too small." She frowned to herself and said, "Hmm. Avoidance?" or something like that.

Denny had said "zoo" in a way that should have made fire alarms go off in my head. And Althea was right about this avoidance. Denny avoided most things he didn't like, and he'd avoided himself right out of the arena and into the woods, I'd bet. I mean—I've known my little brother all his life. "It's what you said about the zoo and the scientists, Althea. He wouldn't want his precious griffin locked up and carved into little bits like a frog in biology class."

"We've got to find him, and the griffin, too. I've got a lot of questions to ask you guys, but it's not going to be anything like the questions you're going to get from the police. That trooper that was here this morning is going to be back. So we don't have much time."

"Officer Schmidt's coming back?"

"Of course he is. This is serious, Natalie. Your aunt Matty is GONE! You two were the last to see her. And Natalie . . . her suitcase and coat were found under your bed!" She bit her lip. "I think you two could be in a lot of trouble."

Like I didn't know this already?

"But, Natalie. I am your friend! Remember that! I can present evidence on your behalf. And I will!"

"You don't believe me," I said.

"Of course I believe you!"

Like fun! She thought I was nuts!

"First thing, though, is to find Denny. Second thing is to get some questions answered. Then we'll get help."

"Finding Denny when he doesn't want to be found isn't easy. He's an expert at disappearing."

"If we just called him?"

I shook my head. "Nope, that never works. And he knows every inch of this horse farm and all the places to hide."

"Too bad Mr. Ironheels isn't still here," said Althea. "Historically speaking, Onondaga Indians are superb trackers."

"Brandy," I said in sudden inspiration. "That dog follows him around like anything. And she's a retriever, so she should be able to retrieve, right? Besides . . ."

"Besides what?"

Okay. So Althea thought Denny and I were crazy. If she thought that, things couldn't get much worse. "Brandy talks."

"Brandy talks? The dog? You mean, like . . . a person? Physiologically speaking, that's imposs—never mind."

Part of this gobbledygook had a pretty good question in

it. I thought about it. "Nope. Brandy talks like a dog would talk if a dog could talk."

"You mean if a dog could talk, it wouldn't necessarily talk like a person, it'd talk like . . ."

This was better. Althea and I were understanding each other just fine. "A dog. Yeah."

"So if we can find Brandy . . . ?" Althea asked.

"She might tell us where Denny went."

"Hm," said Althea. Scooter shifted a little under her weight. "So we're going to go out and look for a talking dog, too, huh. Lord! Okay. I guess we better get on with it."

"Yep," I said.

"It'll be easier to look for Brandy on the horses."

"Yep," I said again. "Look, Althea. You've seen the griffin. I've seen the griffin. We both know that the griffin exists. . . ."

"Oh, we do, we do," Althea said, so fast that I was positive she didn't believe me at all and that she thought Denny and I had stolen a Koko-what's-it lizard from the zoo or something, or maybe even a Gila monster. "It's just that . . . well, what if Bart sees us talking to Brandy and asks us what we're up to? Maybe we should just look for Denny and forget about, um, *asking* Brandy what she knows."

The heck with this. I knew what I knew. And that was that somehow, someway, that dog was able to talk, where as far as I knew, it hadn't talked to anyone before in its life. "If Uncle Bart wants to know how come we're talking to a dog, we'll just tell him that we're doing research for your anthropology class. In dog language."

"You've got such a good imagination, Natalie!"

Now, normally, this is a compliment. I looked at Althea pretty hard. I wasn't sure she meant this imagination stuff as a compliment.

"I'm ready to go talk to fifty dogs if I have to, to get good old Bunkie back. And Aunt Matty, too, of course." I squeezed both heels and Mindy Blue began to walk. Althea lifted her reins. Scooter gave a little buck, and then settled right down and we went outside the arena to look for Denny and the griffin.

There's nothing better than being outside on a good horse on a great spring day, even though you have your suspicions that the person with you thinks your elevator doesn't go all the way to the top. Even if you, yourself, are beginning to wonder if you should be carted off to the loony bin at the slightest pretext, pretext being a perfectly good word I'd learned in language arts not three weeks ago. Come to think of it, as far as I was concerned, anyone who could learn and use a word like *pretext* perfectly accurately was NOT bananas.

I hoped.

We rode along not saying much for a while. I whistled for Brandy about every five seconds, but basically, Althea and I didn't say a word. If it hadn't been for the fact that we were looking for a talking dog, a griffin, and a boy who you couldn't trust with talcum powder in case it might turn into something gross, it would have been a great day for a ride.

Uncle Bart owns about one hundred acres of woods. Bridle paths have been cut through them for the people who board their horses. You ride along these beautiful grass highways with maples, oaks, and aspen whispering overhead. It's a little muddy in early spring, but there's a special kind of green in April that's new and makes me think of fresh-washed babies.

The spring green didn't cheer me up for very long. Althea rode Scooter with a big frown plastered on her face when she thought I wasn't paying attention. Now, this frown could have been because Althea was concentrating on riding Scooter. It takes a while for Scooter to trust you, and until she trusts you, she'll up and jump into a creek if she feels like it. There you are, all wet, with the horse back home in its stall before you know it. But it seemed to me that Althea's frown was more like she had a big-time problem to work out. And it didn't take a rocket scientist to figure out this big-time problem must be me.

We were riding along a little creek that eventually ends up in Lake Ontario fourteen miles away when my whistle scared up a bark. We pulled up and stopped.

Althea turned to me. "Does that sound like Brandy to you?"

I whistled again, then called, "Bran-Bran-Brannndy!" which is Uncle Bart's special call.

I got a bark back. Dogs have different kinds of barks, even when they all of a sudden have learned to talk, like Brandy. There's the "get out of my yard" bark, and the "I'm glad to see you" bark. And there's a "danger!" bark. Brandy barked, "danger!" one time more.

Then . . . nothing.

I stood up in the stirrups and looked around. We were in a part of the forest that's overgrown with brush and old trees. The creek wound its way over stones and fallen logs with a secret whispering. I stared into the water. It was dark, muddy with the rains of spring. Strange shapes moved beneath the surface. I smelled cold and damp under the fresh breeze, and the scent of earth, just dug up. The brush to my right fluttered and moved. Mindy jumped a little beneath me. The bush rattled, and was silent.

"Brandy?" I said into the still, dead air.

"Natalie."

Althea's voice was a whisper. "Behind you. Turn slowly."

Carefully, very carefully, I turned Mindy around on the narrow path. The rustling bush bulged. The sound of a griffin's hiss floated up like smoke.

Scooter whinnied, a cry of alarm. Mindy's hindquarters clenched beneath me. I slammed my knees into the saddle just before Mindy whirled and bolted. Scooter plunged and reared. Both horses splashed into the creek. I slipped, one foot out of the stirrup, and fell backward over the cantle, the reins slipping through my hands. I grabbed Mindy's mane. I shouted "WHOA!" A dark brown hand reached up, took the reins, and pulled me to a stop.

"John!" I was never so glad to see anybody in all my life, practically.

John was dressed like always, black hat with a silver band, deerskin jacket, and his long black hair tied in a ponytail. I straightened up on Mindy Blue and took a couple of breaths. John smiled a little bit, held his finger to his lips for silence, and splashed to the the creek bank, hauling Mindy Blue behind him. Althea was busy with Scooter downstream.

"What's going on?" I whispered. He held up his hand, meaning "wait a second," and we both turned and watched Althea. From the way the mare was raking the water with her foreleg, she looked about ready to roll in it. Some horses like to swim and some don't. Scooter was one of the swimming types of horses, and for a few minutes it looked like she was determined to roll over and do the backstroke.

Althea clucked and nudged Scooter's sides with the calves of her legs again and again, holding the reins to the side and squeezing with both her legs, which is the signal to back up. Scooter tossed her head, snorted, and danced around in the creek. Horses are smart, but not in the way that people are: they like to do one thing at a time. There was Scooter wanting to swim, and Althea telling her to back up, and Scooter couldn't decide which to do first. Finally, Althea got the mare's attention. She settled down and dropped her head and Althea walked her out of the creek to where we were standing.

"She rides well," John said to me in an undertone.

"What spooked them?" Althea asked in a normal tone of voice.

John hushed her and said in a real low voice, "Dismount. And come. Quietly."

John was wearing his rubber barn boots, which made no noise on the forest floor, but then, he's a quiet sort of person anyhow. We got off our horses and tried to follow him just as quietly, but it's pretty hard to be silent when you're hauling a couple of huge horses through the bushes.

It was spooky, picking our way through the woods. I was concentrating so hard on making no noise that at first I didn't hear it.

Mindy Blue heard it before any of us. We came through the trees into a small meadow. There were early wildflowers in the short grass. The new leaves made the sunlight green-yellow under the trees. Mindy stopped, her ears pricked forward, a startled expression on her face. You know that a horse is startled when it plants its front feet smack on the ground, arches its neck, and stares straight ahead with its lower lip hanging open, which is what Mindy Blue did. John was in front of us. He held up his hand to stop. I said, "Whoa" to Mindy Blue even though she'd already whoa-ed, and listened hard.

There was a crackling, snapping sound, like flags flying in a breeze.

I peered through the trees to the meadow. Then I shouted and practically wrecked everything.

Denny was on fire!

CHAPTER

SEVEN

DENNY WAS ON FIRE IN THE MEADOW! I COULD JUST SEE the tufts of his red hair, sticking up over the green and yellow flames. I shouted, "DennnEEE!!" again and stood frozen like a Popsicle. I had to save him! Mindy Blue whinnied just like she was saying, "My goodness, what's this?" and whirled around. I unfroze and leaped toward Denny. I ran smack into the mare and fell flat on my face. I scrambled up and stared so hard my eyebrows hurt. I could see Denny's face through the curtain of snapping light. Green and yellow *fire*? But there was no noise, no smell. Those flames engulfing Brandy and Denny were an illusion! Magic! I shouted one last time: "DENNY! Get out of there!"

The green-and-yellow blaze snapped like a popgun and disappeared. A column of black smoke trailed in the air. Denny sat there cross-legged. He waved his arms like a seagull landing and grinned. Jerk! My bozo brother was just fine and driving me berserk on the slightest pretext, as usual.

"Did you see it?" I demanded. "The magic fire?"

John pushed his lips out, smiled, and didn't say a word. Althea took a big breath, shook her head, and screwed her face up.

This was it. I *was* going nuts. Well, it had *looked* like Denny was on fire, which is why I'd shouted. But of course, the horses weren't scared, just curious, and a real fire would have sent them bananas. Plus, John Ironheels sure wouldn't have stood by and watched my brother burn, so it just must have been that my nerves were, like, totally shot. Denny and Brandy sat there, a normal boy and his normal talking dog.

I tried again. "That's what spooked the horses!" I said. "The fire! You didn't see it?!"

"Fire," echoed Althea. "Oh, Natalie! The si-kosis is progressing!" Or something like that. She put her hand smack on my forehead.

"Feverish," she said to John Ironheels. "Positively. She is NOT responsible."

"You just don't want to believe it," I said. "You don't even want to see it! It was right there in front of us!"

"I'm an anthropologist. I'm trained to be scientifically objective. And you're feverish!"

Oh, sure! I was furious, not feverish. I marched right over to Denny, dragging Mindy Blue behind me.

"Dennis Carmichael Ross!" I demanded. "What *are* you doing?"

"*You're* not Mom," said Denny, like this had anything to do with anything. "And Ike doesn't want them there. Tell 'em to go away."

"Well, Ike didn't let them see anything anyway. They think we're crazy, or Althea does, anyhow." I grabbed him by the ear and looked him over pretty well.

There weren't any burn marks on him, but his face was all over black powder.

"What happened to the fire?"

"What fire?"

"No fire?" I asked. "Where d'ya suppose *this* junk came from?" I dragged a tissue from my jeans pocket, spit on it, and scrubbed at the powdery mess on his face. Althea and John came up softly with their horses. John squatted down on his heels, his face shaded by his big black hat. Althea shifted nervously from one foot to the other. I can't say as I blamed her for being nervous. The grime didn't improve Denny's face any. It had done something funny to his eyes, too, making them red-rimmed and weird.

Denny squirmed away from the face washing and hollered, "Leave me alone!"

"You'd better be darn glad I'm not leaving you alone. We've got to get you back to the barn, and Ike, too. Where is she? I mean he? I mean it?"

"Gone," said Denny smugly. "I told it about di-sek-ing and it left."

"Gone where?"

Denny shrugged.

"Why don't you explain a little of all this?" John suggested. "Who's Ike?"

"There's really nothing much to explain, Mr. Iron-heels," said Althea, babbling. "Just some . . . some foolishness that Denny made up. And Natalie's encouraging him in it, for some silly reason." She laughed like a plate breaking: ha! ha! ha! "It doesn't have to do with Ms. Carmicheal's disappearance at all! No! Besides, they *are* only children. They aren't responsible!''

Children!

She reached out and wiped some of the black stuff from Denny's face with a shaky hand. ''He's hot, too!''

Well, naturally. I mean, the kid had just been in the middle of a fire.

''I think the very very best thing we could do would be to take them right back to the farm and maybe give them an aspirin. Or . . . or . . . a cold pill.'' She shrugged and went ''ha-ha'' again. ''They think they're seeing spirits!''

Think! So much for anthropologists and scientific object-whatever: like, Sudafed's going to keep me from seeing griffins?

''Althea, I, too, sensed a spirit,'' said John, looking as uncrazy as anybody can. ''When we picked you up on the train. And a dream came to me, last night. Of the Turtle, and its Egg.''

''The Turtle?'' Althea's face lost some of the worry.

I didn't know beans about this Turtle, but it must have meant something to her.

She went on, ''Anthropologically speaking . . . that is, the Turtle is, well, the creator of the universe, right? I mean from the viewpoint of the Seven Nations.''

''This is correct. The Seven Nations, as you know, are the original tribes of my people. The Seneca, the Huron, the Onondaga are among them. We believe that the Great Spirit came to the Turtle and breathed into it the means to create—the earth, water, air, and sky. And its Egg is the Treasure at the Heart of the World.''

I shot my fist straight up in the air and shouted, ''YES!''

Finally! Another clue! I pulled that good old paper right out of my jeans pocket to give to John.

Althea jumped forward like maybe the paper was my confession that Denny'd chopped up Aunt Matty and stuck her in the Cuisinart, but I grabbed it back and gave it to John. Thing is, she didn't know John like I did. I mean, who was the person here that'd spent every single summer since I could *read*, practically, talking to John? Who knew that *John* knew more about Indian magic than anybody? Me, that's who.

"The Turtle's Egg is the Treasure at the Heart of the World. Oh, bliss!" I said.

And *finally,* I got to explain about the griffin!

"I see," said John, when I'd finished.

"And when I asked old Mrs. Feather how to unmagic the griffin, that spell you have is what she gave me." I sat next to John and hugged my knees. "Does it make any sense to you?"

John read carefully, then closed his eyes and thought.

"The thing is," I said, before he opened them again, "I figure that the 'Chimney' is Chimney Bluffs, right? And you just said the Treasure at the Heart of the World is the Turtle's Egg, or whatever. I figure we need to take the griffin to that spot and then . . . Well, that's the hard part. I don't know what to do then. I don't know how to unbake the cake."

"The cake?" said Althea. She had this very—how should I say it—exaggerated—that's it—*exaggerated* look of patience on her face. "You can't unbake a cake."

"This is true," said John, reopening his eyes. "And this is what Denny has said? That the griffin has come together like the ingredients in a cake?"

That part worried me. That's no exaggeration. "How do you unbake a cake, John?"

"Well, you don't," said Althea tartly. "Not if you believe the laws of Therm-All Dynamicks," or something exaggerated like that. "You can't transform matter that's past-dependent."

Excuse me? I must have had this exaggerated look of surprise on my face because John said, "What she means, Natalie, is that the only thing that will unbake a cake is to turn back time. You must go back to the period *before* the action transforming the matter occurred to put it the way it was. You must go back in time."

I got about four words in ten out of this sentence, but the four I got were "go back in time."

"How come?" asked Denny.

"Because it's the way the world works!" Althea snapped. "Therm-All Dynamicks explains how things are made. How matter is formed."

"What's 'matter'?" asked Denny, the eternal snoop.

"Matter is . . . is *stuff*." Althea waved her hands around. "Stuff is molecules, atoms. Matter. Everything's made of matter. One of the things that *isn't* matter is magic. A griffin, for example, is a biological impossibility."

"Perhaps," said John mildly, "and perhaps not."

"The thing is," said Althea darkly, with a gloomy look at me, "Natalie has spent every summer since she was a child listening to your tales of Indian legend, Mr. Ironheels. She's clearly very intelligent. And assuming that something dreadful *has* happened to Ms. Carmichael . . . well . . . it'd be awfully easy to make up this . . . this . . ."

"Fairy tale?" He looked at her from under the brim of his hat. "What are you suggesting actually happened?"

"I don't know!" Althea sat down in the grass and drew the ends of Scooter's reins through her hands over and over again. "Ms. Carmichael may have had a heart attack. Or a stroke, and lost her memory. For all I know, she could have fallen into the East River! It runs right by their apartment! And the shock to kids of this age? It must have been terrible. I don't believe a word of this business about the griffin and neither will the police. And that state trooper's coming back, and when he does come back, he may even have the FBI with him. We've got to do something to save Natalie and Denny from them!" She turned to me, grabbed me by the shoulders, and said, "Natalie, please, please! Tell us the truth! I know you couldn't have done anything wrong. Maybe you were just confused. I'm sure you didn't know what you were doing! But you have to tell the truth now! *What did you do to Aunt Matty?*"

It hit me like a brick. Gob-smacked *three* times in one day. I was right, right, right. And here I thought she was nervous about Denny with that weird look on his face. Nope, it was *me* she was nervous about. She thought I was a murderer! Not just a person who might make up kid stuff, but a deep-down, to-the-bone kind of crazy person who'd maybe stuffed Aunt Matty into our building incinerator.

Terrific.

John reached over, wiped his finger down Denny's cheek, and rolled the powdery mess around his fingers. "Soot," he said. "From a fire. Do you see?"

He placed his hand on Althea's arm softly, like you'd pet a scared cat. "There are things in this universe neither you nor I can understand immediately, Althea. Do not dismiss what you cannot taste and feel. Not yet. Believe. Believe and you will see!"

"That's not all, Mr. Ironheels!" Althea leaned over and whispered in his ear.

"Oh?" John reached over and ruffled Brandy's ears. "Is this true, Natalie? That Brandy can talk? Or perhaps I should ask Brandy herself." He scratched under her chin.

Please, I thought. Please! Say something, Brandy, even if it's "Where's breakfast?"

Brandy looked at Denny. He scowled. I swear he shook his head 'no'!

Brandy's tongue rolled out. She panted like anything. Her ears flopped forward like any old dog. She patted John's knee with dog pats, using her front paw like Dad's garden rake. She whined.

But she didn't say a word. Absolutely *nothing* broke the silence, except the wind messing around in the tree branches.

"Well?" said Althea in this "see what I mean" voice.

Maybe, I thought, the ground would open up like a big huge mouth and swallow me right up. I would just sink right down into a nice cave under the meadow and nobody would ever see me again.

"Denny," I said, desperate. "You tell them. Tell them about old Mrs. Feather. About the griffin. And Brandy!"

Denny cocked his head at me. Then he cocked his head to the other side and looked out of the corner of his eye. For a second, just a second, I could swear that Denny's marbley blue eyes turned black and beady.

Griffin's eyes!

"Old Mrs. Feather," said Denny, far away like.

"The magician? Tell them about T. E. About the powder! About turning Aunt Matty into the griffin!"

"Awwkkk!" said Denny. And then: "Scraaaw!"

"Oh, great," said Althea. "This is just *swell!* Bird imitations!" She muttered that word *si-kotick* again, stomped forward, and picked Denny up. "You, young man, are coming back to the farm."

My teeth were chattering so hard I could hardly get out my question. "Where's Susie?"

"Eeeepp, eeepp!" said Denny. He ducked his head. He chomped on Althea's arm with a birdy peck! She dropped him. He laughed! A griffin's laugh! Beside me, Mindy Blue gave a nervous snort. I patted the mare's neck with a shaking, sweaty hand. Horses hated griffins! And ponies did, too! "Your pony, Denny! What happened to her?"

Denny crowed like a rooster, "Back-to-the-barn. Back-to-the-barn. Back to-the-barn!" Then he hopped around on one foot.

"I'll put him up on Scooter and get him home," said Althea. Her words clipped like a pair of scissors. "We'll look for Susie along the way."

"The pony knows her way home," John said calmly. "Do not fear for her. And I do not think, Althea, that the mare Scooter will accept your burden. At least, not at first. Horses must become accustomed slowly to certain types of magic."

"What do you mean?" Althea demanded.

John waved his hand at the horses. Both of them were sweating. The whites of their eyes showed like marshmallows. They backed up the length of the reins away from Denny. Scared. They were scared.

And so was I. Just like the mares, I backed away from this short person with the red hair and freckles hopping around like a chicken. "Can't you SEE!" I shrieked. *"That's not Denny."*

"Calm," said Althea frantically, "we are all going to remain calm."

John nodded. "You are right. That's not Denny. That is Ictinike, the manitou. The trickster. Ictinike, one of the twelve guardians to the Other World." He held his arm out to the thing—it wasn't Denny and I wasn't going to call it Denny—like he expected it to land on his deerskin sleeve.

"Come, Ictinike," he said.

Denny hopped a little ways away.

Then John began to sing, high and thin, all the time walking toward it. You could practically hear the drums in the song, which was sort of "HI-yah-yah-yah, HI-yah-yah-yoh, Hi-YAH, Hi-YAH." Like that. Over and over.

Denny hopped. John sang. Denny began to hop in time, thumping one sneaker down and then the other. "HI yah"—thump!—"yah! HI-yah"—thump!—"yah!" Over and over again.

The fire that wasn't fire came back. Slowly. It ran around Denny's feet like water let out of a cup. It swam up his leg. Coiled around his T-shirt. Like a big wide snake.

Brandy howled. The horses pranced. John sang.

Me, I couldn't breathe.

"My goodness!" whispered Althea. She grabbed my hand tight. I grabbed back.

The fire licked Denny's face, twisted high ... and the griffin's beaky eagle's head flickered on and off Denny's shoulder like an old-time movie. John's song got louder. Brandy stopped her musical howl and began to bark each time Denny's sneaker hit the grass. Brandy spoke through the bark, I could swear it: "Come, One! Come, One!" or something like that. A wind came up from everywhere, from nowhere, blowing my hair, singing in my ears. It was hard to tell the words.

The meadow rocked to the song John sang. The green-yellow flames shot skyward, a tornado of light! That same white light, like a star, like falling into the moon, that white light that had burst in the kitchen at home, and it burst here, in the meadow. Like the biggest, grandest, most incredible waterfall you've ever seen or heard or felt.

Mindy Blue nudged me with her nose, a hard nudge like she does when she wants a carrot. I turned to the mare, Althea's hand in mine. The wind was blowing so hard my ears stung. Mindy looked at me, her brown eyes bright and sad and eager all at once, and said, "Whhhhh-ooonnnn!" and I screamed, "What, girl? What?" and she said. "The One!" in a whooshy, horsey voice that left me gob-smacked for sure.

Then, KaBANG! The wind stopped. The light winked out. Mindy dropped her head and looked like a regular horse.

Everything quit. And it was quiet. My heart was beating so hard I thought I'd throw up.

The griffin sat there! On Denny's shoulder!

"Welcome, Ictinike," John said to the griffin.

"Oooo aWAY!!" the griffin snapped, which I figured meant "go away."

"Go away!" Denny repeated. I looked. His eyes were a regular blue again. Then I looked at Althea with a big smile. I couldn't help it. I know you're not supposed to, like, gloat, or anything, but jeez! This tutor'd spent days thinking I was a mass murderer or some kind of geeky kook, and here was the griffin big as life and twice as real!

And Brandy'd talked! Even Althea must have heard Brandy say, "Come, One," even though it might not make a whole lot of sense to humans.

Althea was the color of cottage cheese. "From a physics standpoint," she said, "this cannot happen. Matter cannot be transformed in this way."

John, who was as calm as anything said, "Sit. And we will ask the spirit."

"Ho," said Althea, like someone'd punched her in the stomach. "Ho." She sat down real fast and dropped Scooter's reins in the bargain. I picked them up so that the horses wouldn't take off and head for the barn, but Scooter and Mindy both started to eat grass, calm as you please. They'd been scareder of griffin/Denny than of a tractor trailer and now *it* didn't bother them at all. But that's horses for you. Go figure.

John sat down in front of the griffin, crossing his legs. "How can we help you, spirit?" he asked, as nice as pie.

"OoooWAY!" The griffin hopped forward in the grass and looked down shifty like. Its beak chittered, Snap-snap SNAP! It dived for a bug and ate it.

"Tell it to stay away from my brother," I said, just to make sure. I mean, Denny was hard enough to live with without being possessed by a mythical monster every forty seconds. "As a matter of fact, why did you possess him in the first place, you?"

"—aan't aLLKK!" growled the griffin.

"You can't talk?" I said. "You're talking just fine now!"

"Eeeak! Eeaak!"

"Beak," said Denny. "It can't talk because of its beak. It can't make the right sounds."

Well, this made sense. But that was still no excuse for possessing a six-year-old person, and I told the griffin so.

Denny rolled his eyes, like being possessed was no big deal, and said, "Can we go home, now? I'm hungry."

"In a minute, Denny. I want to make sure this thing knows to leave us alone."

Althea laughed. Not a normal "ho-ho-ho" but a squeaky, gaspy "a-HUH-huh!" that wasn't real normal, if you get my drift. I patted her on the back. "You'll get used to it."

Althea put her head down between her knees.

"We are forgetting," said John in his mild way, "about your aunt."

"And Bunkie!" I said. Is this typical, or what? Magic turns you all around so that you forget the real stuff, like where this griffin had put my good old cat. "Where are they, you?"

"—on," snapped the griffin.

"On what?" I examined its leathery wings. "On you?"

"On. On! ON!"

"Gone," said Denny. "Ike's says they're gone."

"No kidding! Well, we want them back, griffin!" I put my hands on my hips. "Right now! You've been hanging around, listening. You know what's going on. The police are after us. And they won't quit until Aunt Matty comes back. So. Give!"

The griffin made a very rude noise, like "Phhuutt!" Honestly, this griffin was worse than Denny and the Hammerlich kids—who I absolutely hate to baby-sit—put together.

"Then I guess we'll just haul you off to Chimney Bluffs

and drop you in the lake. That's what the clue means, doesn't it, John? That the Treasure at the Heart of the World is in the lake?''

"That's what it means," said John. "But the manitou spirit must be willing to give up its earthly body. The manitou who is the griffin must agree."

"OOO!" howled the griffin. It swiped its wings back and forth a couple of times and flew up into the tree overhead.

And it didn't take a big-time anthropologist to know what THAT meant! No! The griffin refused to go!

CHAPTER

eight

JOHN TRIED TO TALK SOME SENSE INTO THAT GRIFFIN. Hard cheese. No soap. I stood there, watching. Ictinike refused to do a thing until Denny chirped to it, and even then, it grumbled like a Disposall with a fork in it.

Me? I just sat there having a major stress attack.

I mean, here I thought I'd solved all these problems. John Ironheels had read old Mrs. Feather's clue, and sure enough, we had to throw this griffin into Lake Ontario, just like I'd thought. I'd thought that was one problem fixed. We'd even figured out where the Treasure at the Heart of the World was for the griffin to guard. I thought once the clue old Mrs. Feather gave us was unraveled, we'd get Bunkie back.

Even the problems I hadn't counted on back in Manhattan were fixed up. Althea knew I wasn't Notorious Natalie, the Mass Murderer from Manhattan. So far so good. And while we were taking rests from talking to that stupid Ictinike, John and Althea told me they were both going to help us with Officer Schmidt. Everybody agreed that we would keep this whole thing the most major secret ever. The last human being that should know anything was a policeman. So, hooray. I didn't have to worry about getting arrested, or Denny being the death of some poor child psychologist, at least not right away.

But here was the griffin sticking its little claws in. It refused to help us unmagic it. I mean, the stress I had wasn't from being bored, that's for sure. It was from being FRUSTRATED! You'd think that this griffin problem would be getting easier instead of harder, but nope, no such luck. Just one darn thing after another. I didn't have a clue about how to unbake this cake. That would take magic. And this griffin was not about to let us use *its* magic to blast itself out of existence. Who could blame it, really?

So where was the magic going to come from?

I stood there thinking about all of this while we tried to get Ictinike to have some sense. The conversation would have been pretty hilarious if I hadn't been so mad about losing my cat. And Aunt Matty, of course. First I tried, then Althea tried. All the stupid griffin did when we asked it to agree to unmagic itself was shriek "... o, ... O, ... O!"

Even John had had it. "Denny," he said in his quiet way after this huge long frustrating time, "*you* must talk to Ictinike."

"Why me?" Denny scowled. Even Denny wasn't rude enough to say "you do it" to a grown up, but I could tell that's what he was thinking.

"Don't you *want* T. E. back?" Althea asked.

"O!" Ictinike shrieked. It hopped on the branch and squabbled with itself. Denny blinked and said, "Yeah," to the griffin, and refused to say anything to us at all. I was standing close enough to look at Denny's eyes.

Did a part of the griffin still lurk there? Like a mouse in a hole? I wasn't sure. But there was something wrong with him, that was for sure.

John sang to the griffin a little bit and it finally came down out of its tree and sat on the sleeve of his deerskin jacket. But it was grumpy, that's for sure. John's Indian songs worked to coax Ictinike just like I used to coax Bunkie to do stuff. But there was no way to *make* a cat do things like sit or stay if it didn't want to. John sure couldn't do a darn thing with that griffin.

This was serious.

We had to figure out how to get around this Therm-All Dynamicks and turn back time. And as far as I could see, the only way to do that was magic. Magic from the griffin.

I felt like I was never going to get to the end of this. Denny said about six hundred times how hungry he was, so Althea and I decided to take him back to Uncle Bart's and think things through. John took the griffin and said he'd met us at the farm after dinner. He needed to think some, he said, and then we could develop a plan.

So Denny hopped onto the saddle with me, and the three of us trotted back to the barn. Brandy clumped along right beside us. When we got there, I got more stress. Susie the Shetland was standing outside the gate to her pasture eating grass with her bit in. She should have taken off like a souped-up Harley when she saw Denny. Ponies are basically short criminals in horse suits. But nope, that pony raised its head, snorted "howdy" to Denny, and walked right over to him. I shot a fast look at Althea. She hadn't heard it, thank goodness. I mean, she'd barely recovered from the

shock of meeting a Biological Impossibility. Telling her
what I suspected now about my little brother would have
put her right over the edge.

Althea helped us put away Susie and the horses. We took
off the saddles and bridles, washed their noses and faces
with a damp sponge, and brushed down the rucked-up hair
where the saddles and girths had been. Then we picked out
their hooves with the hoof pick, and turned them back into
their pasture until it would be time for evening feed. *Then*
Althea told us we had to study! In the middle of this huge
crisis! Stress, stress, STRESS!

We got lunch, at least. Althea let Denny make tuna melts
with Doritos smashed on top. Then Althea forced us study
Therm-All Dynamicks. We'd have to learn *something* other
than magic, she said. Something we could actually tell our
parents about. If we didn't, she'd never get a tutoring job
again in this life. This unbaking-the-cake problem with the
griffin was supposedly a perfect opportunity to learn physics.

So we learned about physics.

First off, Althea said all the stuff in the universe is called
matter, which, when it moves, gives off energy. Matter is
made up of molecules. Molecules are made up of atoms.
Atoms are made up of other stuff that gets smaller and
smaller until you get to a quark. Which sounds like a duck,
but it's not. She said there may be matter smaller than a
quark, but nobody knows for sure. Anyhow, this matter
stuff starts out very neat and tidy and then it instantly starts
to fall apart and gives off energy. Like, *immediately.*

The Second Law says it:

This neat and tidy stuff falls apart. Count on it.

Ho! I already knew *that* Second Law. Denny's room at home starts out all neat and tidy Saturday mornings after he cleans it. By Saturday night it is one big mess. Count on it.

This Second Law of Thermodynamics (it turns out this word is spelled like that) made so much sense to me that I asked Althea about these First and Third and Fourth Laws, thinking maybe they would explain other things I'd been wondering about.

Denny piped up and wanted to know how many of these laws there *were* because it made him sick at his stomach just to have to figure out this Second Law and he wanted to go outside and play.

I was getting very, very suspicious of my little brother. I kicked him to shut up and listen. There was a secret in this physics. I was sure of it. Denny knew it. And for some reason, Denny didn't want *me* to know it. I just had this feeling, like I get at the beginning of the "X Files." You know your parents wouldn't let you watch if they were home to turn off the TV. But you watch it anyhow. You have to. And you can't sleep for a week. I had to know more about this physics. Even though I might end up being scared for longer than a week.

Anyhow, it turned out there are Four Laws of Thermodynamics.

The First Law is:

Stuff starts out all neat and tidy. It moves all the time.

The Second Law is:

Stuff keeps ON moving toward being a big mess.

The Third Law is:

This moving stuff *always* goes from neat and tidy to a big mess. (It never goes back to neat and tidy.)

The Fourth Law is:

Stuff always has temperature. It's either always hot or always cold. There's never *no temperature at all*!

So I finally understood about unbaking the cake. The First and Third Law explained that stuff only goes in one direction, from neat and tidy to messy. The Second Law explained that stuff keeps ON going from neat and tidy to messy. And the Fourth Law meant you can never *stop* stuff from moving into a mess, much less make it go backward into neat and tidy.

So, all of us—the whole *galaxy*—tramps along on this ten-million-mile car trip that only goes one way and never stops!

There we were! Stuck! No way to turn back time. No way to get Bunkie, Aunt Matty, and T. E. out of that griffin.

Althea drew little molecules and then atoms on a board. They looked like the Tinkertoys Denny had when he was four years old: little balls with rods sticking out that attached the balls to each other. When you baked a cake, Althea said, the flour molecules rearranged themselves around the sugar and egg molecule so you got a new cake molecule.

"How do you rearrange the molecules back?" I asked.

Althea sighed and shook her head. "There's a relatively new science called nano-technology. Theoretically, we should be able to rearrange molecules if we just knew the exact nature of the rods attaching them to each other. But theory is a long way from the practical. Theoretically, you should be able to achieve absolute zero-degree temperature. But practically speaking, you can't."

Unless you used magic.

Which meant—but that's why I was scared. I was so scared I didn't want to think about it. We had to have the kind of magic that would do what this nano-technology should be able to do, and rearrange the atoms and molecules.

Althea rolled her eyes when I explained these laws back to her and went "No, no, no," but, hey. Tutors can't know it all.

"Stuff is matter, right?" I said. "Stuff is the atoms and molecules that make up everything in the world."

"Well, yes," said Althea, with a sort of gob-smacked look on her face, "but . . ."

"And you said that these atoms and molecules move all the time to make energy. When they move, it's like rubbing your hands together. Moving makes heat. And the atoms and molecules never stop moving, right?"

"Right so far. On a very basic level, of course."

I rubbed my hands together until they were hot. They cooled off right away. I held my hands up. "Where did the heat go? These laws say the heat floats off into the air. The heat keeps on falling apart and getting cooler and cooler and cooler, but the heat never gets to no temperature at all. Right? It always has some temperature."

"Umm. Not exactly. But close enough."

"If matter *got* to no temperature at all, that means it wouldn't move, right?" I said.

"Simplistically speaking," said Althea, "yes."

"Could you give matter a shove backward then?"

"Theoretically speaking, yes. But not using the physical laws of this world, that's for certain."

"Magic doesn't behave according to the physical laws of our world, does it, Denny?"

Denny went "Phhuuutt!" just like Ictinike.

Althea sighed. "Now, anthropologically speaking—"

What about just *regular-like* speaking, for goodness sakes!

I interrupted, which was rude, but this was important. Aunt Matty was at stake. I was beginning to understand that Denny himself was at stake, too. "Suppose we could make the griffin have no temperature. If we could make every single little molecule and atom in it *stop,* then we might be able to shove it backward and rearrange its molecules?"

Althea started blabbering on about ants! Cohere-ants, or something like that. I said I thought this was physics, not biology, and she rolled her eyes and stuck her hands in her hair, asked the ceiling how come she had even *started* this lesson, and huffed, "We will now turn to geography."

Geography! When I was just about to figure what to ask the magic to do?

"We'll wait for Mr. Ironheels," Althea said firmly. "No offense, guys, but look what happened when you two messed around with magic the first time."

Well, we studied geography. Althea made us recite the fifty states alphabetically and didn't let us out until both of us did it right. Yuck.

Denny and I finally got *some* peace after our millionth time of getting all the way to West Virginia without a mistake, and we went on down to the barn.

"Want to play Spiderman?" asked Denny, who thinks this Superhero is, like, King of the Universe. Is this just like an six-year-old, or what?

"We've got important stuff to do, Denny."

"Like what?"

"You'll see."

"Like *what*!"

"A test. You just wait."

"We just HAD a test!" Denny yelled, like I was going to make him to eat raw liver. "I want to play Spiderman!"

"Not that kind of test. It's something to do with Ictinike." I looked at him. My little brother. Freckles. Red hair. Innocent—but squinty—little blue eyes.

And very, very dangerous.

Uncle Bart was bringing the horses in for evening feed, so I had to wait to give Denny this test. Which was okay by me, because I was scared to do it. The test, I mean. I love evening feed. Denny and I help with evening feed every chance we get. At evening feed, the horses are nice and sleepy after hanging around outside all day. The stalls have been raked clean of manure and fresh bedding has been put in, so the barn smells great. And horses love eating oats for dinner, so they are very happy. We helped put Mindy Blue and Scooter and Susie in their stalls and Denny kept bugging me and bugging me about what was this important stuff we were supposed to do. I had to wait until Uncle Bart brought in the last horse and left the barn to wash up for our own dinner. Then I told him.

"I want to talk to Mindy Blue."

He made a face, rolled his eyes like a goop, and said that was stupid, horses couldn't talk, I was stupid, ya-ta-ta-ya-ta-ta.

"Denny," I said. I was very serious. I think it scared *him*. "You *know* what we're going to do. And you *know* that I know. Right?"

I dragged him to the front of her stall. Inside, Mindy Blue was eating her hay with this very nice sound: *chomp chomp, chew-chew*. I slid open the door and we went in.

Mindy Blue jerked her head up and looked at us, then stuck her nose back into her hay and grabbed another big bite. I watched Denny out of the corner of my eye. "Well?" I said finally. "Do it, Denny. Cast a spell to make her talk. Right now."

I'd finally figured it out. Denny was a magician.

CHAPTER

nine

DENNY PATTED MINDY BLUE ON THE FLANK, WHICH IS THE hip part of a horse, and said, "Hello, girl," acting like I hadn't said a word.

Mindy kept on chowing down, like I hadn't said a word, either. You can watch a horse chew away like anybody's business, but you never see it swallow. I stood trying to catch Mindy Blue swallowing, then decided to stop being a coward and said, "Well, Denny?"

"Well, what!"

"You know very well, 'well, what!' I want this horse to talk to me! Right now!"

His eyes slid away from mine. "You're nuts!"

"I'm not nuts! You're the one who's the magician. And you make her talk right now!"

John pushed the stall door a little wider. "May I come in?"

Mindy swiveled her ears forward and chuffed a sound like "Whoof!" But that good old mare moved right out of the way, even though it was getting kind of crowded with all three of us in the stall. John ran one hand down the length of her foreleg and ended up with a pat on her shoulder. She liked this, you could tell.

"You've discovered Denny's talent?"

"Denny's talent?" I closed my eyes. Shuddered. The mere thought of Dennis Carmichael Ross loose in this world with magic at his fingertips was enough to make you faint dead away on the spot. Talent's like a thing you do that's cool. Aerosmith. Now Aerosmith's got talent. "I'd call it a good old curse, that's what I'd call it."

We both looked at Denny, who was picking his nose. Gross. I grabbed his hand and made him wipe it off on his own jeans.

"He IS a magician, right? I mean, the animals talk around him. Whenever they've talked to me, it's been because Denny's sent a message, or because he's right there where they are, and the magic sort of spills over. And I've been thinking about how the griffin got made in the first place. I've been thinking about this a lot. If I'd gotten that talcum powder from old Mrs. Feather, and chanted all those words, there never would have been a griffin." I took a deep breath. "Do you know much about magicians, John?"

He didn't answer me right away. Just took the lead line he'd been carrying and snapped it under Mindy's halter. "Sorry, old girl. We're going to have to interrupt your dinner. You kids ready?"

"Ready for what?" I asked.

"We've got to go to Chimney Bluffs. Tonight. Althea's going to go with us. She's got the tents and food ready. I've talked to Bart. Told him I'd promised you a moonlight ride last year, while I was still working here. Told him I didn't want to renege on my promise.''

''What's 'renege'?'' asked Denny.

''Go back on it. I didn't want to go back on my promise. Even though I don't work here anymore.'' He motioned for us to go out of the stall. We did, and he followed us leading Mindy Blue. In the aisle, Althea was tacking up Scooter. Scooter's ears were laid back in her cross way, which meant she wasn't at all happy about having her dinner interrupted.

''Bart is so worried about losing the farm to the Loomises that I think he's glad to be alone tonight.'' John sighed. ''Not much I can do to help him except this to get your aunt back. I've wanted to help. We've been friends a long time.''

''You're not mad about being fired?''

John smiled. ''Well, I won't be fired if we can get your aunt back, will I? She's good at business. She'll find a way out of Bart's financial troubles. If we can find a way to get her out of hers.''

Without my even telling him, Denny went down the stalls to Susie and started to get ready to go, too. John and I were alone. I picked up a currycomb and brushed Mindy's back. Maybe John would talk to me now. ''Why do we have to go tonight?''

''There's two reasons we have to go tonight. The first is, Ed Schmidt is going to be back at the farm tomorrow. The second is Ictinike herself.'' He stopped talking and brought me my saddle. I got it up over Mindy Blue's back and tightened the girth.

''Ictinike's a she?''

''Ictinike's a she,'' John agreed. ''And a very angry,

very determined she, at that. The manitou are strange be-
ings, Natalie. And of the twelve, Ictinike may be the worst.
She is the trickster. She finds this world a wonderful place.
As I do. As we all do. She does not want to leave it. And
the longer she stays, the more her power grows. If we do
not attempt the magic tonight, when the moon is full and
at its height, she may be too strong for us tomorrow. You
saw what happened in the meadow this afternoon. The second time her magic enveloped your brother—well, we all
I saw it. If she were to get an opportunity to envelop him
yet a third . . . I believe we will have lost all hope of getting
your aunt Matty back. But that's not what I fear most.''

The barn was quiet, expect for the stamping of the horses
and the low murmur of Althea's voice as she talked to
Denny about tacking up. I didn't want to ask this question
but I did. ''What you fear most?''

''That Ictinike will want an earthly body to possess while
she is in this world. And that Denny is her choice.''

The barn grew cold, or so I thought. I shivered, and
swallowed hard. I knew it. I knew it. That's what had
scared me. Scared me silly. ''Denny . . .'' I croaked. I
trailed off, and didn't say a word after that. Denny. My
dorky little Spiderman-loving brother. Possessed by the
griffin. Forever. I flipped the bridle over Mindy's head. I
shivered. ''What are we going to do?''

''Our magic must be powerful enough to turn back time.
I know such magic lies at the Heart of the World, Natalie,
but what I know, I know from study. From learning from
my fathers, and their fathers before them. I do not have—as
I believe Denny must—a special talent. I do not know how
to invoke it.''

''Can Denny do it?''

"He needs to be powerful enough to call Ictinike back to her proper role as one of the twelve manitou guarding the gates of heaven. I don't know if he can do it."

"Will it be dangerous? Will it be dangerous for Denny? Because it if is—"

"I don't know," he interrupted gently. "Denny does not know himself. When the moon is at its height, I will sing into being a wind. And the wind will part the water. What happens after that?" He shook his head. "That is the limit of what I know. Perhaps Denny will know. We must risk it. We have no choice."

We took the horses out into the Yard. John's big black gelding, Dark Moon, was already saddled and waiting for us. A paint packhorse named Susie Two stood by, loaded with camping gear. John's horse is really called Dark-Moon-That-Drifts-On-Water in Indian, but John just calls him Moon. Moon's what Uncle Bart calls a bombproof horse. You could practically set a firecracker off under his nose, and he wouldn't budge an inch. But Moon was restless, as the sun set, and the darkness rose over the far horizon. The knitted saddlebag over his right hindquarter bulged in and out.

Ictinike. Which was why even Dark Moon was nervous until John talked to him and calmed him down.

Althea brought Scooter out, and we mounted to ride.

Then? Disaster! A pickup truck screeched into the Yard. A huge *beep* made Scooter jump and shy. The headlights swept the Yard. They winked out. Two figures piled out of the truck. The Loomis kids. I should have known.

"Ironheels," said this Jeff, with no respect at all, "saddle our horses. Bart told us about this camping ride. We're coming along."

"It will be a long hard ride in the dark," said John mildly, "and it may be coming on to rain."

"So?" said Brett, so rude you would not believe it. "You wait for us."

Jeez! I looked at John and whispered, "Should we leave Ictinike here? Go tomorrow, when they aren't around?"

John shook his head. "No time. We must trust in the One."

The One what? That's what I thought Mindy Blue had called, in the middle of the magic storm: the One. So I asked John, and he said, real low, "We believe that the Turtle is the One who made all. The One Great Spirit who gives life. The One who gives animals speech. The One who carries the Treasure at the Heart of the World. And it is guarded by the manitou." And that's all he'd say about it since Brett kept whining about what were we "saaaying"? It was hard to think, with that yowling banshee.

Well, we hung around the yard until bratty Brett and her bozo brother fussed with their horses and got ready to bust up our trip. One bad thing was that Brett's horse, a pretty chestnut named Fancy, didn't want to be anywhere near Dark Moon and that griffin. By the time that Jeff and Brett were saddled up and ready to go, Fancy had sweat running down her withers. Brett got on and slapped her with a wicked-looking crop. Fancy shook and trembled so much that I wanted to smack Brett with the crop. But John looked a warning at both me and Althea, who was just as mad as I was. We kept out of it. The Loomis kids were *finally* ready. We rode out of the Yard and into the depths of the forest.

There's a poem I read in English lit. about the moon being a ghastly galleon riding on a wine-dark sea. Or something. It was like being in that poem, riding out from the farm in the dark, except it wasn't ghastly, it was totally great. The air smelled fresh. The trees were silvery in the dark, lit by the sailing moon. The whole thing made me want to yell, just to make a good noise. I would have, if I hadn't been so worried and, like, stressed out to the max.

But I *was* worried and I *was* stressed to the max. I was so scared for Denny that I couldn't stop thinking about it.

We rode along with no noise but for the jingly sound of the horses' bits. John kept us to a steady trot. We'd reach the lake in about two hours. John said that we would have to try the magic when the moon was at its height. It was low in the sky right now because the sun'd just set. It would be at its height in five hours or so. At midnight.

The trail to Lake Ontario runs through a whole bunch of apple orchards, across a couple of main roads, then through apple orchards again. Those farmers who grow all that fruit must have planted the trees with horses in mind. Four-foot paths run between the rows of trees so the trucks can come in and load up apples from the pickers. The trails are as nice and flat as you please.

The moon was beaming all over the place. We rode steadily on through these trails. The only part of the ride where we had to stop and wait was when we crossed the main roads. And at that time of night, there wasn't a lot of traffic, only a few cars and once in a while, a semi tractor trailer. But you would have thought we were in the middle of Times Square at rush hour, the way that Brett complained. First it was the dark, which you get when you go on a moonlight trail ride, for Pete's sake, and then it was crossing the roads in "all that traffic!" and then it was woodchuck holes. Whine, whine, whine!

And then, of course, poor old Fancy was nervous about the griffin, so she danced around a little bit and Brett made it worse by yanking on her bridle. Our horses had got used to Ictinike—a horse can get used to a tiger if it's around it long enough, especially if it trusts its rider—so *we* didn't have any trouble. But Brett just made Fancy's nerves worse and worse.

We got across the highway just fine until Brett yanked on that poor mare's bridle once too often. Fancy hollered, reared up, and Brett fell off with a crash.

We all hopped off and got Brett to her feet. She was yowling like anything, of course. John went to Fancy's head to keep her quiet while Althea checked Brett over to see if she'd broken any bones.

"Just you wait!" Brett screeched. "My father's going to hear about this. He'll put this whole stupid barn out of business!"

"Your father can't call in the mortgage," said Althea, who was losing her cool pretty fast. "Bart's been paying it every month, just as they agreed."

"He can TOO! My father says that anyone who doesn't use his imagination in business is a dope. And he can make that dope pay anytime he wants to. My dad fixed it that way."

"Bart is not a dope," said Althea between her teeth. "And if your father were a good man, he'd be using his imagination to help Bart, not put him out of business."

Honestly, I think good old cool Althea might have pasted Brett one right in the snoot if John hadn't come up. He held Fancy's bridle in his hand. "Be quiet, or your horse will run away, Brett. Look. This is the way to assemble this bridle. Do you see? You've attached the bit directly to the reins. Every time you pulled on the reins, the bit hurts the horse's mouth. You must fix the right way to assemble the bridle in your head. Imagine the right way to do it before your fingers place it together. If you keep the right way to do it in your mind's eye, you won't make as many mistakes.''

I didn't hear the rest of all that went on. I was thinking, and thinking hard. About imagination. About keeping the right way to do things in your head. About that weird nano-technology.

By the time I'd thought it all out, we were back on the trail.

I had all these questions boiling around in my brain. The most important one was: What kind of magician was Denny?

I rode up beside him in the dark. "Denny!"

"What?"

"You remember when you scattered that powder over T. E. What did you see?"

"Huh?"

"Did you see the griffin in your mind? Did you . . ." I fumbled around, because I wasn't sure how to say this. "Did you know what you were going to make with the spell?"

He sighed like this was this stupidest question he'd ever been asked. "The powder made everything all spots. The spots looked like the things Althea drew for us today. Lots of little spots. I just made the spots move around until they were the griffin."

Molecules! I knew it! "Could you turn the griffin into little spots without the powder?"

He shrugged. "I guess."

It had to be more than a guess. It had to be right. Because if I was wrong, life was going to be pretty scary from now on. Ictinike could grow in power and take over my little brother once and for all. And I was darned if I was going to live with a griffin in that little apartment.

But if I was right, Denny was the kind of magician that could take things apart—right down to their molecules and atoms. If I was right, he could rearrange the way these atoms and molecules were put together. We could get Aunt Matty and Bunkie and T. E. back. We could make Ictinike jump right back in the lake and guard the gates of heaven or whatever with the eleven other manitous. Things would be the way they were before.

Brett's father was right, in one way. You had to use your imagination and and NOT do things the way other people did. And Althea was right: you had to use that imagination to help people. If Denny had the right picture in his head, he could reassemble my cat (and Aunt Matty of course), just like Brett was supposed to have reassembled the bridle.

If I could just get Denny to use his imagination! I must have made a noise like a sob or something. John pulled Dark Moon up a little and dropped back beside me. I could just see his outline in the dark.

"Anything wrong?"

I wasn't sure I wanted to talk. Not just yet. So I changed the subject and said in this low voice, "Why are the Loomis kids so awful?"

John thought about this for a second or two. "I think," he said, "it's because they have nothing to love."

So there we were, right back on the subject, because I did love my horrible little brother. Love was why we were in this mess to begin with. Love makes things very complicated.

"I've figured out how Denny could unmagic the griffin, I think," I said. "But I don't know if he *can* do it." I explained about how Denny could maybe *see* the molecules and atoms that made up the griffin and Bunkie, too. "But how am I going to make him see them in his head? He's six!"

I could feel John smile at me, if you know what I mean, because I sure couldn't see him.

"Very powerful emotions. Like love. They will help Denny remember. You must help him, Natalie. By recalling what he loves about T. E., Aunt Matty, and you."

John began to sing. It was the same kind of song he'd sung to the griffin in the meadow, but quieter. Softer. I don't know if it was all that fresh air, or John's song, or the fact that you can't go around in the world being stressed all the time without getting tired, but I began to get sleepy. Behind me, the awful Brett even stopped whining, yawned, and for a while the only sound we heard as we jogged and jogged was John's soft song.

The hours passed by like nothing at all. Then I felt Mindy begin to move uphill. John's song trailed off, like a breath on a wind, and I came out of my dozy feeling.

The air smelled like daffodils. We rode up over a rise. The lake glimmered under the starry sky. It spread before us. Vast. Deep. The waves washed against the shore like the flick of a gigantic tail. The stars picked out the points of the foamy white tops. At first, I thought the lake was silent, maybe because it looked so awesome in the dark under the moon. But the water had a voice of its own, like a whispering giant. "We'll make camp here," said John.

Camping with horses keeps you busy, which is good, because I didn't have time to think. Thinking just brought the scared feelings back. We unsaddled the horses and rubbed them down, checking their hooves for stones and dirt. They each got some oats. John and Denny climbed down the cliff to the shore and brought back water for them to drink. Then we put on their hobbles and turned them out in the grass to feed. Hobbles are good when a horse is used to them, because they can move around but they can't gallop off home, leaving you stranded fourteen miles from nowhere.

We pitched three tents. We toasted hot dogs and cooked baked beans over the campfire. John hummed under his breath all the while. Brett kept yawning and yawning. I was feeling a little bit sorry for her, because she could love at least her horse, not to mention her own dopey brother, but there she was, selfish and miserable. I think she loved her hair more than anything.

I'd figured out by now that John's song was a sleep song. It was working. The trouble was, it was working on everybody, me included, and by the time Althea, Denny, and I rolled our sleeping bags in our tent, I could barely keep my eyes open. The Loomis kids took a tent each. John rolled himself into this fabulous patterned blanket near the cliff. I decided that the best way to keep awake was to pinch myself, so I pinched and pinched and went to sit beside him.

"There is no need to watch with me," John said. "I'll wake you when it's time."

"I want to watch, too," I said, but the song he sang got into my brain. Even though I pinched my knee like anything, I fell asleep beside him.

John was gone when I woke up. The moon was obscured by clouds. The sky was the darkest it had ever been that night. I scrambled to my feet. I was stiff from lying on the ground. I must have made a groan or something. A shape moved out of the dark and touched my arm. I jumped about a foot.

"Come," John said. "It's time. Wake Denny, only." He carried his embroidered saddlebag over his shoulder. I heard the griffin grumbling inside, "—o—o—o." She must know what was coming.

"I promised Althea!" I whispered. "I told her I'd wake her up in time."

John's teeth showed white in his face when he smiled. "You will not be able to wake her. It will not be permitted."

Permitted by who? I thought. The One that John talked about? The One that took the shape of a giant Turtle, that helped animals to talk? I crept through the dark toward our tent. I sure wanted to see this Turtle.

I could just make out the shapes that were Mindy Blue and the other horses. Mindy Blue called to me with a soft whiffly sound that meant, "Who's there?" I called back softly, "It's me, girl," then crawled into the tent. Althea was deep asleep. Denny was wide-awake. His eyes glittered. Were they black or blue, my brother's eyes? I couldn't tell.

I grabbed his arm and it felt like it always felt—a little sticky, because six-year-olds are always sticky, no matter how many times you make them take a bath—and he said, "We do it now? Cool!" I shushed him.

I shook Althea. Althea slept on. I shook her again, harder.

"She won't wake up," Denny said in his normal voice. "The Loomis kids won't wake up either. Not unless John wakes 'em."

"Why?"

"Because it was his spell, of course."

We didn't say much, John and Denny and I, as we picked our way down the cliff to the shore. But Ictinike did. Ictinike growled "—o—o—O!" the sound getting bigger and bigger, like the thunder from a storm.

We reached the rock-filled shore and stood there, gazing at the water.

John faced the waves, raised his arms, and sang. A soft wind rose like sigh, blowing the clouds across the sky like leaves at the end of autumn. The moon came out like a silver orange, full and round and glowing.

John stopped singing. He looked at Denny. "Are you ready?"

"Sure!" said Denny, normal as anything. As though we weren't stuck on the shore of a lake a million miles from nowhere, about to turn back time.

John swung his pack to the ground. The lump inside that was Ictinike looked bigger to me, much bigger. John unfolded the saddlebag and stepped back. He began to chant. A deep, rhythmic chant. It beat, beat, beat against the night like a drum.

Ictinike came out. Slowly. Bigger than I'd ever seen her before. As big as Denny, as big as me. She grew as I watched her. Her dragon's tail snapped. Her giant beak opened and shut with the sound of a deathly machine. The moon shone on her wicked eyes, which were fierce with a terrible fire.

The wind whipped the waves. They drew back, back,

back into the lake. Then the water swept back and crashed against the shoreline with a violent wash of spray. "Denny," I said. "Denny. Think about how Ike is made of little spots. Make her into little spots."

He turned to me. Denny's blue eyes that had been black, black, with Ictinike's spirit were green now. Green with magic.

I tried like heck to use my imagination. What would bring the picture of T. E. and Bunkie to Denny's mind? What would make it clear as clear to him? What would make him want to bring my cat and his parakeet back? John said love was a powerful emotion, and love would help him remember.

What did *I* remember about that dumb parakeet?

"Think about T. E. and how you fed him stuff in the morning."

Denny shrugged. I should have known that wouldn't work. Half the time I have to feed T. E.

"Remember when Dad brought T. E. home? And you left his cage door open and he hopped right onto your bed and slept by your pillow?"

Denny rubbed his nose and nodded.

"And remember when Bunkie let T. E. eat her kitty chow? Remember how they hang out together waiting for us to get home from school?"

"Yeah!" Denny said.

"And remember how we didn't think Aunt Matty was going to make it last Christmas and she got there late and brought T. E. that cool new bird cage? The wicker one with the door he could open and close himself?" I touched his shoulder. "You do want them back, don't you, Denny?"

Denny made that bratty face, the kind when he thinks

it's cool to drive you crazy. There was one last thing I could try. I loved Denny, right? And the little brat probably loved me.

"Denny," I said, "Darn it. I miss Bunkie. I miss the way she sleeps on my foot." Tears hit my nose all of a sudden, like they do when you don't want to cry, but you might have to. "Darn it, Denny." I hadn't counted on sobbing like a fool, but there you are. Love's weird.

Denny kissed me, the little jerk. And then he began to chant in his high voice. He stood next to me, his body rigid, his head thrown back. He spread his hands. A faint green glow came from his fingertips.

Ictinike shrieked again. She made her way back and forth, back and forth, beside the water, shaking her head. Her clawed feet struck sparks from the rocks. The lake got wild. The spray dashed high, a hurricane of water.

"Go hooommme!" Denny cried. "Go hoommme!" and the green fire flew from his fingers and wrapped around the griffin's body.

The wind whipped wilder and wilder. And then the griffin began to dissolve in a billion tiny specks. Ictinike was a swirling, spinning mass of glowing spots. Denny's hair blew like fire. The waves reached for him, a giant palm of water. I leaped forward and grabbed him. His arms were there, under my clutching hands, but I couldn't *feel* them.

"Denny!" I screamed into the wild, tormented wind.

And he was there, my brother, his hand in mine, his hand that wasn't hot and wasn't cold, but no-temperature, no-weight at all.

Ictinike's terrible beak opened. She reached for Denny like she would swallow him whole! I got scared. I pulled Denny back. We had to get back up the cliff to safety. John and Denny and I crawled up the cliff, Denny still chanting that no-word song. When we reached the top of the cliff, there were the horses, their heads raised to the moon. Eyes dark and wondering, while the wind and water whipped their manes, they stood with eager faces: Dark Moon, Mindy, Susie, Scooter, and the others.

Below us, Ictinike stalked by the water. Her snaky tail lashed back and forth.

Denny stuck his hands in his jeans. He looked down at Ictinike and said, "Go *home!*" The griffin was a whirling pillar of green fire. Behind her, the lake and the sky began to glow with a different light. Gold and red. Two moons shone before us! One moon rode the sky, a flood of golden white. The other came from the lake like a mammoth fire-struck rose.

The water of the lake foamed. Some *thing,* some giant was coming from deep below the water. It was coming in answer to Denny's call.

Ictinike spread her wings and shrieked a third time, with a cry to split the waves and make the night sky shake.

Denny took his hand from mine and walked to the edge of the cliff. I was right beside him.

A Turtle came out of the water. The biggest Turtle I've ever seen. Bigger than the Empire State Building. Bigger than the sky itself. It was beautiful. Its shell was an emerald, carved with strange spells and letters. A scarlet ruby bloomed on its back. The red moon I'd seen in the water. The red rose that had come from the water. I looked into that jewel. The warm flame of its presence throbbed like a giant heart.

It was the Treasure at the Heart of the World.

Ictinike stared at the jewel on the Turtle's back and froze.

Denny shouted. Denny . . . *pushed*!

The Turtle raised its head. Black eyes. No-color eyes. Every-color eyes looked into mine. The wind went away. The waves dissolved to level silver.

The wise, kind eyes of the Turtle blinked shut.

The water from the lake drew back, leaving a shining path. The griffin stood at one end. The Turtle waited at the other.

Eleven columns of whirling, spinning, misty green-and-yellow light formed along the path to the great Turtle. The pillars spouted high like green-and-yellow volcanoes. Six spun on one side, five spun on the other. Closest to the Turtle on the right hand side, where the five manitous twirled like giant glowing tops, was a sixth dark space. The space for Ictinike.

Beside me, the horses breathed. Mindy Blue said, "Go!" Dark Moon whispered, "Go!" Susie, shouted, "Go!"

The water lapped around Ictinike's glittering starry tail and around her gauzy wings. Her body was a transparent wash of all the colors in the world.

Denny *pushed*!

Ictinike went. Step-by-step. Down the path to Ruby Heart that rode the Turtle's back. She passed the columns one by one.

She hopped on the Turtle's back with a "Scraw!" and a shout of "Yes!" and a final shout of "Mine!" and cocked her fierce black eyes at us.

Then the pillars sank with the Turtle and its glory. The water closed over the whole shining fantastic mess.

And the night was very quiet.

CHAPTER

TEN

SO MUCH FOR MAGIC. WE SAT MOST OF THE NIGHT ON that dumb cliff, and not only did those horses go right back to grazing and never said a word, but my good old cat never showed up. Neither did Aunt Matty.

I couldn't believe it. Everything had gone the way it was supposed to. Denny had frozen Ictinike and pushed her backward. I kept asking him and asking if he'd kept the memory of Bunkie and T. E. all the while he pushed that griffin back home, until he got mad and did his "shut up" routine. Denny's "shut up" routine basically means he answers every little thing you say to him with "shut up!". He thinks it's hilarious. Then I asked him if he was still a magician. I mean, it was like totally possible that this was a one-time thing and that I wouldn't have to worry about him, like, turning fire hydrants into panthers or something seven days a week. All he'd say to that was "huh?" so maybe that was one thing that wasn't going to give me stress.

I was not glad about the rest of it, though. This nano-technology magic should have worked. Plus, these Laws of Thermodynamics were a big joke and bogus to boot. No cat. No parakeet. No Aunt Matty! The heck with stupid physics. The only good thing was Ictinike. That griffin was gone for good. I knew that. That Turtle was just the sort of reptile a person could trust.

Denny fell asleep without John singing a single note of a sleep song, and I guess I must have, too, because the next morning the sun smacked me right in the eyeballs. I rolled over, got up, and was the stiffest I've ever been in this life from sleeping on the ground.

Denny lay curled up on the ground, his fist tucked under his cheek. I was about to nudge him awake with my toe, and then I thought, Jeez! It might be sort of stupid to wake up a magician too fast. And then I thought, Nope, no way, José. I wasn't going to spend the rest of this life afraid my baby brother was going to call up giant reptiles from the sewer system or something.

I tickled his face with a piece of grass. "Hey!"

Denny rolled over, yawned, and rubbed his face with both hands, smearing the dirt around. Then he said, "Cut it out!" and tried to sock me in the stomach. His eyes were, like, a totally normal blue.

So *that* was all right. This magician stuff must have been a one-time thing, like measles.

We went back to camp. John was crouched over the campfire, cooking bacon that smelled absolutely delicious. The horses were waiting to take their turn at the water bucket. Althea crawled out of the tent, saw us, and ran over.

"I missed it!" she said. "What happened? I can't believe you didn't wake me up!"

"I tried," I whispered. "The magic wouldn't let me!"

She looked sad. "It would have been interesting, from an anthropological standpoint, that is." Then she looked around and whispered, "Where's your aunt Matty?"

I shook my head.

"You mean it didn't work!"

"Guess not."

"Where's Ictinike?"

I pointed to the lake. "Gone. To guard the Treasure at the Heart of the World with her eleven pals. *Now* what are we going to do?"

Brett and Jeff were coming out of their tents making these disgusting whining noises like "Where's breakfast?" so we had to drop the subject. I didn't mind them as much as before. I mean, I had this hunch that we were the only friends they had.

But I couldn't let them in on the secret, of course. So I didn't get a chance to talk to John, or Althea. And when we rode into the Yard about three hours later, I was, like, totally unprepared for what I saw.

Officer Schmidt's cruiser was in the Yard. There was a black car parked right behind the cruiser, and some guy in a dark suit and a tie talking to Uncle Bart.

The FBI.

That wasn't the worst part. The worst part was standing right next to Uncle Bart. Mom and Dad! Back from Paris! "Mom!" shouted Denny, the idiot, and took off like a rocket on Susie.

I cantered Mindy Blue after him and whispered, "Okay, kid. You let me do the talking, understand?" Denny just jumped off his pony and ran over to Mom and Dad. I got off Mindy Blue with a *little* more respect than my dopey little brother and kind of walked casually over to them.

So we hugged and kissed for a while and Mom smelled as good as ever, and Dad was great, and then I drew this big breath, finally ready to talk. It was all going to have to come out, and I'd be locked up with that child psychologist for sure. Mom said, "You both look wonderful, sweetie! But of course, we came back for nothing! Madeline's back!"

And then the Keuka Taxi Service drove right into the Yard and Aunt Matty got out, mad as fire and soaking wet. She had T. E. in a cage in one hand and was holding good old Bunkie in the other. She handed Denny the cage and glared at me.

"T. E!" Denny screamed, just like he hadn't totally abandoned his parakeet for that griffin the past few days.

"Yo, BUNK!" I said, and grabbed my cat, casual like. I buried my nose in her plump little neck and sniffed her good old fur. She smelled great, if a little weedy. She climbed up on my shoulder and sat there. Purring like anything and rubbing her head along my chin. I was the absolute least stressed I've been in years.

And I was *really* happy.

"Well!" said Aunt Matty after dinner. "The effects of the amnesia have worn off! I feel like my old self again!"

We were all sitting around the table. Bunkie was nice and warm in my lap. Aunt Matty was dried off, and she'd changed into clean clothes from Mom's suitcase. I'd made spaghetti, partly because I like the way I make spaghetti, but mostly because if I was busy in the kitchen with Mom and Althea, Aunt Matty couldn't get me alone. I wasn't all that sure she'd forgotten about temporarily being a griffin.

"So," said Dad, "you really don't remember where you were for two days, Madeline? I mean, not until you came to yourself while you were swimming in the lake?"

Althea coughed so hard Uncle Bart had to pat her on the back.

"The FBI agent may have been right," Aunt Matty said. "Stress. Stress can bring on all kinds of problems, and a temporary amnesia is only one of them. I've been working too hard, I suppose."

I could tell Aunt Matty something about stress, I guess!

"But why when you had this—this amnesia did you take the cat and the parakeet with you?" asked Mom.

Aunt Matty's cold eyes rested on mine for a long, long minute.

Oh, no. Oh, boy. Oh, rats! She *knew*!

"Well," she said finally, "I guess I just wanted the company."

Nobody said anything for a second. I thought Althea was going to bust a gut from not laughing.

Aunt Matty swept the table with her famous glare. "You know, I've been thinking, Alison. You and Dave might be right. I've been pushing it too hard. It might be time for me to relax a little bit. Maybe take Natalie and Denny to Yellowstone National Park. Or something. So we can all be alone. Just the three of us. Would you like that, kids?"

Jeez! I automatically reached over and clamped my hand over Denny's mouth, just in case he decided to shout something like "NO! She's trying to kill us because we turned her into a griffin!"

"Natalie?" said Mom, with this "aren't you going to be polite?" tone to her voice.

"Um, thanks, Aunt Matty, but I've got a lot of stuff to do at school. Like geography, for instance."

Althea leaned into her plate and snickered.

"Well," said Aunt Matty, "we'll see." She looked at me for a long, long minute. "Dave, you and Bart and Denny get the dishes. Natalie? Let's walk out to the barn. I'd like to see how the horses are doing."

"It's my turn to do the dishes," I gabbled. "And then I've got to get Denny ready for bed—"

"Now," said Aunt Matty.

So we walked out to the barn. My heart was pounding. My hands were kind of damp. I slid them on my jeans leg and said, "Would you like to go for a ride tomorrow?"

"Down to Chimney Bluffs, for example?" Aunt Matty's voice was icy.

"Well, there or—"

"So I can see the *Palm of the Hand*?"

I turned around and faced her.

She knew! She knew that she'd spent three days as a griffin! I kind of looked at her sideways. She was smiling!

"Actually, I have to go into the village tomorrow and buy out Bart's mortgage from that shyster Loomis. So we'll skip the horseback ride. Maybe later. Okay?"

"How . . . how much do you remember?" I asked in a hushed voice.

"All of it, actually." She put her arm around my shoulder. "It was . . . interesting."

"Did you . . ." I swallowed. Now that she knew, I could ask what I'd been dying to ask. "Did you see the Turtle? Up close?"

Her face went soft. Those practically permanent cross lines between her eyebrows went away. She looked . . . lit up . . . sort of. "Oh, yes. I spoke to the Turtle. The part of me that was buried in Ictinike rode the Turtle's back." She didn't say anything for a few seconds. Whatever she was remembering must have been the best. It must have been the most beautiful, too. "As a matter of fact, that's why I want to speak with you alone. I have a message from . . . *it*."

"It? It's not a him or a her?"

"It's not anything like a human being, Natalie. It's just *it*." Her eyes got a little weird. Sort of soft. "That Turtle. So filled with love, Natalie. There's a lot about life that I've missed. But!" She dusted her hands together in the old bossy way. Love doesn't make you somebody different, I guess. Just happier. Which is okay by me. "*But* there is a bit of information you need to know. About Denny. For the future."

"He's a permanent magician," I said. "Jeez! I *knew it!* Aaagh!"

She laughed. And let me tell you, I have never heard Madeline Carmichael laugh before. At least not soft and happy like that. "A wizard, really. A magician is more like John. A person who has the art to do small things, like call the breeze. A wizard is a much mightier thing. But it may not be as bad as you think. You must be his guardian, Natalie, at least until he reaches an age where he knows how to work for good, each and every time. And, like most guardians, you'll have both good and bad times handling it." She was wearing a striped shirt of Mom's that buttoned to the neck. She unfastened the top button and pulled out a necklace. My pearl necklace, the one I'd given the griffin to guard three long days ago in Manhattan. "This is what Denny will use to make his spells, at least for now. You are to be caretaker of it, to pull it out when there's need."

"Need?" I said doubtfully. "What kind of need?"

Aunt Matty smiled. "Oh, there'll be adventures to come, Natalie. You're a great kid. You're going to handle them well."

And she hugged me. Aunt Matty, the Dragon of Wall Street, was, like, being a loving sort of person!

Well, there wasn't much else to do, was there? So I hugged her back.

Jeez!